Brander Matthews, George Henry Jessop

A Tale of Twenty-Five Hours

Brander Matthews, George Henry Jessop

A Tale of Twenty-Five Hours

ISBN/EAN: 9783337022778

Printed in Europe, USA, Canada, Australia, Japan

Cover: Foto ©Andreas Hilbeck / pixelio.de

More available books at **www.hansebooks.com**

A Tale of Twenty-five Hours

BY

BRANDER MATTHEWS

AND

GEORGE H. JESSOP

NEW YORK

D. APPLETON AND COMPANY

1892

Prefatory Note.

In a different form and under another title this story was published four or five years ago in an American magazine and also as one volume of a British series. Carefully revised by its authors, it now appears for the first time in its proper proportions.

B. M.

G. H. J.

Contents of the Thirteen Chapters.

A Tale of Twenty=five Hours.

CHAPTER I.

MR. PAUL STUYVESANT'S SITTING-ROOM.

M R. PAUL STUYVESANT'S bachelor apartment was on the seventh floor of a tall building overlooking a broad square almost in the centre of New York. Years ago the broad square had been named in honor of an American president; and the tall building, only recently remodelled, now recalled the title of an English duke. Its lower floor, level with the street, was a single huge store, wherein one of the chief jewellers of the world vended his glittering wares. Most of the rooms on the sécond floor were leased by a sporting club, composed of fast and fashionable

I   I

young men, many of whom, having taken
to horses, were making ready to go to the
dogs.   The upper floors were devoted to
apartments for bachelors; and into these,
as into the monastery on Mount Athos,
no women were allowed to enter save
when one of the inhabitants asked a married sister to matronize a flock of girls
who came to have a cup of tea osten-
sibly, and in reality to investigate the
bachelor's den.

From the seventh floor the outlook was
wider than it was below.   Paul Stuyvesant knew what he was about when he
took rooms at the top of the house, and
he had never regretted his selection.
What he sought especially was quiet;
and this he had found.   Indeed, he had
found more—a certain faculty of ab-
stracting himself from the busy life of
the city beneath him—a power, as it
were, of cutting himself off from the rest
of the world.

This morning there was neither dust
nor noise.   Almost the first snow-storm
of the winter had come and gone during
the night.   A white blanket covered the

cornices of the building across the way, and the cross-pieces of the giant telegraph-poles were encrusted with sparkling crystals. The thin layer of snow clogged the car-tracks on the street far below, and deadened the sound of the horses' feet. The roar of the traffic of the great city arose muffled; and even the sharp note of the car-bells, which came up clearly enough now and again, seemed farther off than before. Although it was late on Friday morning, there was a hush almost as though it were Sunday. Perhaps it was owing to this unusual calm that Stuyvesant was oversleeping himself.

His apartment consisted of a sitting-room, a bedroom, a bath-room, a tiny hall, and a closet or two. The large square sitting-room had four windows, two looking out to the east and two facing the south. It was a bright and cheerful place, generally; and now, as the slight snow-storm slowly ceased, and the sun gained power to force its rays through the dense gray clouds, this room had a very pleasant aspect. It was such

a room as a man might be glad to enter
and sorry to leave.

When the sun had at last turned itself
full on and flooded the place with its
brightness, a boldly painted portrait
which hung on the western wall next to
the entrance-door glowed with life, and
seemed ready to start from its frame.
This picture was singularly strong in
color, and it had not a little of the mellow tone and golden richness which lend
so great a charm to the paintings of the
great Venetians. It was the portrait of
a handsome man of about thirty or thirty-
two years of age. He was tall and dark;
his countenance was aquiline; his eyes
had a penetrating glance as they followed a visitor about the room inquisi-
tively. To these eyes, indeed, the visitor involuntarily recurred; and he could
find in them a look of curiosity—a quality most precious, and objectionable only
when misapplied to the pettinesses of existence. The impression made by the
picture varied, of course, with the character of those who might look at it.
Most people were pleased with it; most

people, if closely cross-questioned, could
have been made to confess that it looked
as though the man who had sat for it
was pleased with himself.   But so frank,
manly, and engaging was this man as
revealed by the artist that most people
did not give this revelation a second
thought.   The picture was a portrait of
the owner of the apartment, painted by
Charley Vaughn, to whose sister, Kath-
erine, Stuyvesant was engaged to be
married.

On the narrow space of wall between
the two windows opposite the picture
was a tall frame, divided longitudi-
nally into three sections, in which were
diplomas.   One bore witness that the
owner of this department was a Bachelor of Arts, *summa cum laude*, and this
was enriched with the seal of Columbia
College, Novi Eboraci.   The second tes-
tified that the University of Gottingen
had conferred on him the degree of J. U. D.
The third was a certificate of member-
ship in the famous fraternity of Alpha
Omega, the secret society which Stuyvesant had joined in college, and mem-

bers of which he had met all over the world in the most unexpected places.

Between the windows on the southern side was a panoply of arms, or at least what might pass for such at first sight. On closer inspection, the weapons were seen not to be those that are customarily arrayed in trophies. Among half a dozen other unconventional weapons were a cruel-looking gimlet knife and a roughly wrought bowie, on the broad blade of which could still be seen the cross-hatching of the file from which it had been made. This last object of interest had been a present from Charley Vaughn.

Two or three hickory sticks blazed and crackled in the fireplace on the northern wall of the room. On each side of the broad wooden mantelpiece were bookcases packed with solid tomes as high as a man might reach while standing on his feet. Some of these were portly law-books, sedate in their sheepskin coverings. Some were books of reference in German, French, and English. Some were the books that no gentleman's library should be without; but of these there were only a few, and they looked as fresh as when they had left the bindery. On a shelf level with the eye, and within easy reach of the right hand as the owner of the room should stand before the fire, there was a row of books of all sorts and conditions. Some of them had been handsomely bound, and some of them were still in the frail paper covers in which they had been issued; but all bore marks of repeated readings. Chief among them was a set of the complete works of Edgar Allan Poe; the volume most worn was that containing "The Murders in the Rue Morgue" and "The Gold Bug." Next to this stood a paper-covered copy of "The Moonstone," by Mr. Wilkie Collins, and an English railway edition of "A Confidential Agent," by Mr. James Payn. Near these were "The Leavenworth Case," by Miss Anna Katharine Green; "His Natural Life," by Mr. Marcus Clarke; "The Mark of Cain," by Mr. Andrew Lang; and "The New Arabian Nights," by Mr. Robert Louis Stevenson. The "Mémoires de

Vidocq" elbowed half a dozen tales by Emile Gaboriau and Fortuné du Boisgobey; and " Les Morts Bizarres," of M. Jean Richepin, brought up the end of the line.

A broad desk-table was in the centre of the room. Its flat surface supported a student-lamp, and also a large photograph in a velvet frame, with velvet curtains drawn over the portrait closely, so that no indiscreet eye might recognize the features of the lady. Bits of paper of different sizes, each of them having a sentence or two written on it hastily, some in ink and some in pencil, littered the centre of the desk. It might fairly be guessed that these were the accumulated notes intended to serve in the composition of the thick manuscript, the sheets of which were heaped together just under the student-lamp. On the first page of this manuscript was written " A History of Circumstantial Evidence: with an Analysis of its Fallacies. By Paul Stuyvesant, J.U.D., Adjunct Professor of the Canon Law in Columbia College." Apparently the author had been laboring on his book until very late at night, and had gone to bed as soon as he had done his stent of work, without waiting to gather up his scattered notes. Perhaps in this delayed labor might be found the reason why he was sleeping so late this morning.

CHAPTER II.

IT was past ten o'clock when Stuyvesant came out of his bedroom into the parlor. In the strong light it could be seen that the portrait on the wall behind him was a striking likeness, although perhaps a certain dreaminess which might lie latent in the original had been accentuated by the artist. Rich as was the coloring of the portrait, it was not warmer than the flush which arose to the face of the man as he stepped to the table in the centre of the room and took up the photograph-frame which stood there. He parted the velvet curtains, and gazed intently on the face of the woman they had concealed. It was a pretty face, and he looked at it long and lovingly. Then he kissed it once, twice, thrice, and set it back on the table. It was a photograph of Miss Katharine Vaughn.

Although he was a college professor, Paul Stuyvesant was a young man and an ardent lover. Just now his whole thought was of his future bride, and how he might make her happiest. It was because he had lingered later with her the evening before that he had been obliged to work on until far into the night. Fortunately, the fortnight's vacation for Christmas and New Year was not yet over. It was Friday, the 3d of January, and he had no lectures to deliver until Monday. The day was his own, and he might do with it as he pleased.

There was a knock at the door, and one of the janitor's assistants brought in a tray containing Stuyvesant's breakfast, which was the only meal supplied in the apartment-house. The books and magazines which littered a small table in the corner were hastily cleared away, and the breakfast-tray was set down. The attendant laid a letter and the *Gotham Gazette* of that morning by the side of the tray, and left the room.

Stuyvesant took his seat at the table; but before he tasted the golden Florida

2

orange, with which he always broke his fast, he took up the letter. It was from Charley Vaughn:

"THE RUBENS,

"January 2d.

"DEAR POST SCRIPT: Perhaps you may remember that you promised to go with me Saturday to see the new pictures. If you don't recall the circumstance, this will serve to remind you of it; while it informs you that the engagement is off! I can't meet you, because I'm to meet the Bishop of Tuxedo to talk about a stained-glass window for his new church. You know he is a man of the world—they used to call him the Apostle to the genteels—and I think I shall suggest Dives and Lazarus as a subject. With some new ruby glass I have just seen, I can put Dives into a red-hot hell. That's a job that would have puzzled Titian! I rob you, Paul (of an appointment) to pay Saint Peter—that's the name of the new church.

"So long,

"CHARLEY.

"P.S.—I've been trying to read this and it seems scarcely legible. I see I haven't put in the commas and things. Season to suit yourself. I hold that punctuation is the thief of time.

"C. V."

Stuyvesant read this brief letter with some surprise. He did not understand the reason given for the cancelling of the engagement. He glanced again over the letter, and he remarked in it what seemed to him like forced gayety. The humor struck him as artificial. It seemed to him almost as though the note were the result of an effort. In general, Charley was as light-hearted a young fellow as could be found in all New York, and he had a flow of spirits as far removed as possible from any suggestion of strain. And yet this was not the first time that Stuyvesant had seen signs of a certain constraint in Charley Vaughn.

Paul laid the letter on one side and began his breakfast. As he poured out his coffee he remarked that the tray was not quite level; one corner was higher than the other; and beneath it he found a thin little book, inside of which was a bundle of slips of paper. In clearing off the table he had overlooked this. He recognized it at once as the pass-book which he had sent to the Metropolitan National Bank to be balanced, and which he must have taken out of his pocket the night before. The bundle of slips was a collection of the checks which he had drawn during the past six months.

Only half a year before had Paul Stuyvesant opened his first bank-account, depositing the check for the salary of his professorship. Old as he was, a checkbook was still a novelty to him; and it was with a boyish pleasure that he broke the band which encircled the thin bundle and began to turn over the cancelled checks. Here was the very check he had drawn to pay for the engagement-ring he had given to Katharine Vaughn. Not a few of the others could be connected with her more or less directly. There was another, drawn in payment of the little supper after the theatre-party which he had given her, and which Mrs. Duncan had kindly matronized—the supper at which Charley had flirted so funnily with the pretty girl from Yonkers. Yet a third was to the order of a florist; and as he looked at it there arose a vision of Katharine Vaughn as she stood before him at the ball, radiantly beautiful, supremely happy, and holding in her hand the bunch of roses he had provided for her.

As Stuyvesant turned this check over, he took up the one beneath it. He recognized that also, and he knew where the money had gone. The check was to the order of Charles Vaughn; and it had been posted to him only a fortnight before, to pay Paul's slight losses the last time they had played poker. He had been unlucky that evening, and he had not yet forgotten the four deuces with which Charley had beaten his ace-full. He smiled, as the recollection of a good game of poker seems to make most Americans smile. As he turned the check over on the others, he was struck by the indorsements. Most of the checks had been deposited at once by the payees. This alone had apparently passed from hand to hand, almost as though it were a bank-note. There were four names on the back: Charley had given it to M. Zalinski, who had indorsed it to the order of James Burt, and he in turn had passed it along to Eliphalet Duncan. Now, Stuyvesant knew Eliphalet Duncan as well as he knew Charley Vaughn. That a check which he had given to Charley should find its way into the hands of Eliphalet, after passing through those of two unknown men like M. Zalinski and James Burt, struck him as peculiar. M. Zalinski—the name seemed somehow familiar, although he could not place it at once; the handwriting was stiff and foreign: probably the man was a Polish Jew. The signature of James Burt was bold and irregular, as though it was the result of main strength misapplied.

Stuyvesant turned over the rest of his checks carelessly as he went on with his breakfast. Then he took up the *Gotham Gazette*, while he smoked a cigarette with his coffee. The newspaper happened to be so folded that the eighth page was under his eye. He had not more than glanced down the first column before he checked the cup which he was raising to his lips. A curt paragraph informed the readers of the *Gotham Gazette* that the case of James Burt, charged before Police Justice Van Dam with having burglars' tools in his possession, was postponed until the following Wednesday, at the request of his lawyer, Mr. Eliphalet Duncan.

Stuyvesant laid down the paper and stared straight before him in deep thought. He had found, apparently, the connecting link between two of the four indorsements on his check. James Burt had paid it over to Eliphalet Duncan as a retainer. That seemed simple enough. But who was M. Zalinski? And how came Charley Vaughn to be paying money to a man who had dealings with a burglar? These questions he put to himself repeatedly, and he found no answer. Charley was neither eccentric nor fast; and it was no easy task to account for his having passed Stuyvesant's check to a man who had passed it on again to a

house-breaker. The combination of circumstances was singular, certainly, but
probably it was of no significance whatever. Charley had behaved queerly of
late in more ways than one, it was true;
but no doubt he could explain in a few
words this curious linking of his name
with a malefactor's. Paul said to himself that he was attaching too much importance to a trifle, and that a perfectly
innocent explanation would be forthcom-
ing in due time. Of course, if Charley
were in trouble in any way, Stuyvesant
would do all that he could to help the
boy out. Katharine Vaughn was a bond
between them, all the stronger, since the
girl was unusually proud and fond of her
clever, light-hearted brother. Paul was
very fond of Charley for his own sake
also, and he was ready to go great
lengths, if he could relieve the young
fellow from any worry which might be
wearing on him.

For a few minutes Paul sat silently
thinking, and not conscious of the series
of concentric smoke-rings which he was
blowing, one through the other When

his cigarette burned down and scorched his fingers, he aroused himself. Lighting a second cigarette, he took up the newspaper again. He turned it, and on the first page he found this despatch from Paris, set forth with a hydra-like profusion of "display heads:"

"THE EXTRAORDINARY THEFT OF A PICTURE!

"The art world of Paris was thrown into a high state of excitement to-day by a rumor that the great painting of Mary Magdalen, by Titian, had been stolen from the handsome apartment of Mr. Samuel Sargent, the well-known American millionaire and chief owner of the Transcontinental Telegraph Company. This is the great picture which was so romantically recovered two years ago, after having been lost to sight for nearly two centuries. It was painted in Ferrara in 1520 for Lucrezia Borgia, and it had been lost since the beginning of the eighteenth century. It is a single head, treated in the great artist's most glorious manner. Mr. Sargent has been away in

Russia for more than six months, leaving his magnificently decorated apartment in the Avenue de l'Opéra locked up. When it was opened, the Mary Magdalen was gone. It had been cut from the frame. The police do not know when the robbery had been committed; but they say they have a clew to the thieves."

Here followed a brief description of the scene of the crime, with a further account of the stolen picture, including the dimensions of the canvas.

"Now, that is really very curious indeed," said Stuyvesant to himself. "This is the second paragraph in to-day's paper which is of interest to Charley."

Just then there came a sharp knock at the door.

CHAPTER III.

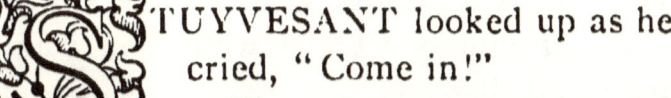TUYVESANT looked up as he cried, "Come in!"

The door opened, and Charley Vaughn appeared. He walked straight to the blazing fire and began rubbing his hands.

Charley Vaughn was a lively little fellow, with curly blonde hair and a quizzical face. He wore a pair of eye-glasses, behind which his sharp blue eyes were never still.

"Is it very cold out?" asked Stuyvesant.

"It isn't the cold I mind," Charley replied, taking a cigarette from a cup of cloisonné enamel which stood on the mantelpiece. "It's the confounded uncertainty of the thing. I'm in Greenland's icy mountains one day and on India's coral strand the next. In the

course of a week Old Probabilities serves
us up a great deal of weather of assorted
sizes: if you don't see what you want,
ask for it."

"If you want a match, you will find a
box on the book-case behind you," suggested Stuyvesant, smiling.

"Thank you," returned Charley
gravely. "Let me beg of you not to
rise. I can help myself. I should hate
to put you to any inconvenience."

He lighted his cigarette, and then took
up a favorite masculine position on the
hearth-rug, with his back to the fire and
his feet well apart. His eyes fell on the
breakfast-tray.

"You got my letter, I see," he said,
watching Stuyvesant closely.

"Yes," answered Paul dryly.

There was an awkward pause for a few
seconds. Charley kept his eyes on his
host until Stuyvesant happened to look
up; their glances met, and the guest, with
a little nervous laugh, dropped his gaze to
the floor.

"I came in to explain how it is,"
Charley began, in a hesitating way, in

marked contrast with his usual glib speech.

Stuyvesant smoked on silently.

"I can tell you how it is," pursued Charley. "I like the Bishop of Tuxedo: he's a white man, for all he's a gospel-sharp. And so I thought you wouldn't mind my postponing our engagement for to-morrow."

There was another awkward pause, and then Stuyvesant said:

"I thought you hated stained glass with a holy hatred?"

"I do hate it, of course; but——"

"But you like the bishop so much that you are willing to make an exception in his favor?"

"Exactly," said Charley, quickly seizing at the explanation obligingly offered.

"Ah!" Stuyvesant rejoined, with significance.

"Now, what do you mean by that contemptible '*ah!*'?" cried Charley with a show of indignation.

"Nothing," answered Stuyvesant, coolly—"nothing much. Only this, in fact, that I heard you say last week that

you would as soon compose music spe-
cially for the hand-organ as make a design
for stained glass, in the execution of
which the artist was wholly at the mercy
of the artisan."

"Did I say that?" asked Charley pit-
ifully.

"I heard you," was the uncompromising reply.

"Oh, well," the artist responded at
last, "if you are going to search my record, and try to pile up petty inconsist-
encies, I shall not say another word. Of
course, there isn't anything to explain."

Here he glanced again at Stuyvesant
sharply; and again Stuyvesant looked up
and caught his eye.

"Can he suspect anything?" thought
Charley. "He studies my face as though
my secret were written there in black and
white."

"What is the matter with the boy?"
was Paul's mental query. "He is not
straightforward with me this morning. I
wonder what he has on his mind?"

"You lawyers are always so sharp,"
said Charley, at last. "You seem to

think you have the whole world in the
witness-box.   By the way, how is the big
book getting on?"   And he made a gesture toward the pile of manuscript on the
table.

Stuyvesant saw his chance, and seized
it promptly.

"It's a long job, of course," he said,
"and I have hard work to get all the material I need.   I think I shall go down
and ask Eliphalet Duncan if he has some
fresher facts for me.   You know he has
been engaged in several important criminal cases."

"Has he?" asked Charley, with indifference.

"I see by the paper this morning,"
Stuyvesant went on, "that he is to defend
an alleged burglar—James Burt."

He never took his eyes from Vaughn's
face, but the face made no sign.

"I believe," continued Stuyvesant,
"that this Burt is a pal of Zalinski's."

"Of Mike Zalinski's?" Charley inquired eagerly.

"That is the man's name, probably,"
Paul answered.   "Do you know him?'

"I've met him," said Charley.

Stuyvesant did not like to push the matter farther. He felt that it was impossible for him to ask Charley what his connection with Zalinski might be. There was something in his young friend's manner which he had never seen there before. It was a vague restlessness—a sort of subdued feverishness.

"Don't you feel well, Charley?" Paul asked suddenly.

"Why shouldn't I feel well?" he replied indignantly.

"I thought you looked worn or worried," Stuyvesant returned. "That's why I asked you."

"Oh, I'm all right," Charley rejoined. "I'm as chubby as a cherub, and as chipper as a chipmunk."

"If I can do anything for you——" began Stuyvesant.

"But you can't," interrupted Charley hastily. "Can you minister to a mind diseased? I mean, can't you be satisfied until I pack myself up in paper-shavings, as if I were imported glass-ware—this side up, with care?" And, as though anxious to change the subject, he went over to his friend's portrait.

"That's not bad, you know, though I say it as shouldn't," he remarked, as he drew off and examined the picture critically. "I don't believe I shall ever get the values better than I did then. The color's pretty harsh in some places, though. But the composition isn't so queer, after all. You see, Paul, you stoop, and one of your shoulders is higher than the other: most people wouldn't notice it, perhaps."

"Thank you," said the subject.

"You needn't thank me," replied the painter; "I saw it plainly enough, and that's why I posed you as I did. I flatter myself that I made Art conceal the defects of Nature."

"Go on," Stuyvesant laughed, "go on! Don't mind my feelings."

"I don't," said Vaughn. "When I stand before a portrait I know no mercy; I forget all friendship; I ignore all the conventions of civilization. That is why I dó not hesitate to tell you that one side of your head is all out of drawing."

3

"In your picture?"

"On your body."

"Now, Charley——" began Stuyvesant, half laughing and half piqued.

"It is the frozen verity," the artist insisted. "You have no right to hold me
responsible for the blunders of Nature.
The most I could do was to try and invent a scheme of color that would distract
attention from the defects of the subject;
and I think I have succeeded fairly well
in that."

"Am I to understand that, if you had
done me exact justice, I should appear on
the canvas deformed?"

"No," replied Charley gravely; "no,
it is not as bad as that. In the main,
you are not much amiss——"

"A thousand thanks——"

"But one side of your head is out of
drawing; that I have said, and that I
stick to! But I doubt if one man in a
million, or even if one artist in ten, would
find it out. You see that there is a glow
to the picture, a richness and a mellow-
ness like those of the best portraits of the
great Venetians. And that is the result

of using the marvellous medium I discovered after I once had a chance to restore a Sasso-Ferrato. I stretch my canvas myself, and I prime it myself, as the old masters used to do. Then I lay on the color with a medium of my own compounding. When I retire from business I shall reveal the secret of that medium, and the whole world of painters will rise up and call me blessed. With that medium and a little touch of a varnish I know, I can make a cow-boy as romantic as a bull-fighter. I can shine up a picture of mine until it glows almost like a Titian."

"Have you seen the *Gotham Gazette* this morning?" asked Stuyvesant suddenly.

"No. Why?"

"There's a cable despatch in it which will interest you."

"Has the Queen at last discovered my genius? Has she cabled to the President requesting him to engage me to paint her portrait?" asked the artist.

"The news does not refer to you directly. No doubt her majesty will send for you some day, and perhaps you will tell her that her royal head is out of drawing too."

"I see that my truthful criticism of your anatomical imperfections still rankles in your shallow soul. Go on with the news. Of course, if it does not refer to me personally by name, I cannot think it important."

"The Mary Magdalen of Titian is stolen," Stuyvesant said.

"They have found that out at last, have they?" was the artist's reply.

"What do you mean by that?" asked Stuyvesant surprised. "How did you know that it had been taken?"

Charley Vaughn looked up, as though in wonder at the other's vehemence.

"I never supposed he came by it honestly," he answered after a pause.

"He?" returned Paul. "Who?"

"The man in whose possession I found it first; in fact, I used to regret that I didn't take it and keep it for myself when I first saw it," Charley replied, and his voice became more enthusiastic as he continued: "You don't know what a marvel it is. Titian never did anything else as good.   The drawing is masterly, and the coloring is incomparable.   I have never seen a picture I would rather steal."

"Are you in the habit of stealing pictures?" asked Stuyvesant grimly.

"No," Vaughn answered as gravely; "but I would make an exception in favor of this one."   After a momentary pause, he added: "Let me see the paper."

Stuyvesant passed it to him, and he read the paragraph slowly.

"I see," he said, as he laid the newspaper down again and lighted a fresh cigarette.   "This time there is no doubt that somebody has carried it off.   The man, whoever he is, has a treasure, but it is a treasure he will have to keep to himself; he cannot show it to his friends; he cannot boast of it; he cannot sell it; he cannot let any one even suspect that he has it in his possession.   I can understand how he feels, poor fellow!"

"Are you pitying the thief?" asked Stuyvesant.

"You are not an artist, and you have never seen that picture, or you couldn't

help pitying a man who had in his possession a gem of the first water, which he
dare not display, and which he can enjoy
only by stealth."

"When did you see it last?" inquired
Stuyvesant.

"I'd sooner tell you when I saw it
first," replied Charley, after a moment's
hesitation. "You know I am almost the
rediscoverer of that picture. I saw it in
the window of a brocanteur, near the
Château d'Eau, in Paris, one day about
four years ago. It was dusty and dirty,
and the frame was almost broken to bits;
but when my eye lighted on it I was fascinated. I went in and asked the man
what he wanted for it. He said he had
just given the refusal of it to a gentleman
who was to return at three o'clock. If
he didn't take it I could have it for a
thousand francs. I examined the picture
carefully, and I felt sure that it was a
genuine Titian, and one of his best. I
tried to beat the man down, of course,
and told him it was impious to ask a
thousand francs for an old crust like that.
But he retorted that I needn't buy it if I

didn't like it, and that, even if I did like it, the other gentleman had the refusal. As I looked at the picture, the longing for it grew on me. In my head I went over a list of the people I could ask to lend me a thousand francs. Of course, I hadn't any money on hand. It was near the end of the month, and I was living on three francs a day, and there was a month's rent due. At last I made up my mind that I would take the picture and the seller with me in a cab to the banker's, and I would vouch for the value of the picture, and ask them to lend me the money to buy it. I didn't dare go away, for fear I should lose the chance. It was not twelve when I caught sight of it, and I waited there until three. Five minutes before the time expired, a gentleman came into the shop, and my heart dropped into my boots, P. D. Q. I knew him by sight: he was the manager of the London branch of a great firm of French picture-dealers. As soon as I saw him, I knew that my chance was clean gone. He paid the thousand francs, and he had the picture put into his carriage. Just as he was driving off, I mustered up courage to ask what he would take for his bargain. I spoke French, but my tongue betrayed me, and he answered in English that he expected that his morning's work would pay a profit of ten thousand pounds—only this, and nothing more."

"Ten thousand pounds?" repeated Stuyvesant. "Is this Mary Magdalen worth anything like that?"

"They sold it to Sam Sargent for three hundred thousand francs," replied the artist indignantly. "That's the sort of thing that makes Communists. I wanted that picture, and I could have appreciated it. Sargent got it, and he doesn't know the difference between Giorgione and Georges Ohnet: he deserved to have it stolen from him. He kept it shut up, so that it was very hard for any one to get at it."

"From the way you received the news, Charley," said Stuyvesant, "and from what you said, I was beginning to think that the theft was some great practical joke, and that you knew the picture was gone some time ago."

"I confess the news didn't surprise me," the artist answered. "A clever man would have no great difficulty in getting into Sargent's apartments while he was away."

"How do you know that?" Stuyvesant asked.

Charley Vaughn flushed up as though he had made an awkward admission.

"Never mind how I know," he answered. "Let's change the subject. Are you going skating to-day?"

"I don't know," Stuyvesant returned. "I am going to call on Kitty at twelve, and if she likes——"

"I see: you will do as you are bid. Happy man, you are under petticoat government already!

> "'Life, young man, is only
>   A slippery sheet of ice;
> No girls there, it's lonely—
>   One girl there, it's nice.'"

And with this he went toward the door.

"Good-morning," said Stuyvesant.

When Charley Vaughn reached the door, he paused as though in doubt. Then he turned, and in a hesitating way and with an obvious effort he spoke again:

"I say, Paul, are you superstitious—like the Irish gentleman who wouldn't commit suicide on Friday because it was an unlucky day?"

"Why?" asked Stuyvesant.

"Oh, I don't know," replied Charley, grasping the door-knob again. "I thought I'd ask—that's all. Some fellows are afraid of doing anything important on Friday."

"I am not," Stuyvesant returned.

"Neither am I," said Charley. "So long! See you later. I really must exude now."

CHAPTER IV

MR. PAUL STUYVESANT PAYS A VISIT.

FTER Charley Vaughn left him, Stuyvesant remained for a minute or two in thought. There was something in the boy's manner that the elder man did not like. There was a certain suggestion of restraint all through the interview. Just what this peculiarity might be, Paul could not precisely define for himself, but it seemed to him as though Charley were laboring under a suppressed excitement. Beyond all question, the young fellow was suffering from some tension of the nerves. And Stuyvesant could not help wondering whether this was due in any way to his relations with the M. Zalinski to whom he had given a check which M. Zalinski had passed to a burglar.

Still turning these things over in his mind, Stuyvesant threw his cigarette into the fire and began to dress to go out. When the elevator came up to take him down he caught himself looking in the broad mirror which filled one side of that aerial vehicle. Unwittingly he had been examining his own appearance in the looking-glass. A sudden blush mantled his cheek; and then he smiled as he thought that six months before he never would have dreamed of looking in a mirror. It was the desire to appear well in her eyes which tended to make a fop of him. He smiled again as he reflected that even the wayfaring man, though a fool, might know that he was going to see the woman he loved.

When he came out on the street a sharp wind struck him, and he set out briskly.

Under the influence of the rapid walk and the bracing breeze Stuyvesant's spirits rose, and he succeeded in throwing aside the vague feeling of depression which had overshadowed him ever since he had seen the name of James Burt on the check he had given to Charley Vaughn. As he breathed the pure air and as the exercise sent the blood to his cheeks, he began to

take a more cheerful view of the matter.
Before he reached the door he was calling
himself a fool for having attached any
importance at all to what was probably a
mere coincidence of no significance whatever.

Mrs. Vaughn's house was on a side-street
only a few blocks above the square which
Stuyvesant's apartments overlooked.   It
was a very little house, barely fifteen
feet wide, trying vainly to make up in
height what it lacked in breadth.   Small
as it was, however, it was amply large
enough for its occupants, Mrs. Vaughn
and her daughter Katharine.   Mrs.
Vaughn was a widow with only two children, Charles and Katharine.   They had
each an income fairly sufficient to satisfy
them if their wishes were modest and
their administration economical.   Charles
had been able to study at the Paris
School of Fine Arts and to spend a year
in Italy, chiefly at Venice.   Katharine
and her mother had always lived together;
and Charles, although he had set up for
himself and had a bedroom adjoining his
studio, was very frequently at his mother's

house.   He was a good son, as Katharine was a good daughter; and the mother and her children lived happily.

Stuyvesant was ushered into a rear parlor, miscalled the library.   In reality it was Miss Vaughn's sitting-room, and it reflected the presence of a young lady of a charming diversity of taste.

As Stuyvesant entered this pretty room of a pretty girl and took a seat amid its characteristic disorder, a bright voice came floating down from the floor above:

"Is that you, Paul?   Oh, I'm so glad! Just wait.   I'll be down in a minute."

A minute passed, and two, and ten— and Paul still sat in lonely silence.   He began to be a little impatient.   He rose, and walked up and down the room three or four times.   Then he took up a magazine, and, resuming his seat, he turned its leaves with indifference.   A paper on "Political Cohesion" caught his eye, and in a few seconds he became absorbed in it.

So absorbed was he that he did not hear the light rustle of a dress as Katharine Vaughn floated airily downstairs. He had his back to her, and she came behind him and clasped her hands over his eyes.

"Guess who it is!" she cried.

"And what reward shall I have if I guess aright?" he answered gravely.

"I don't know," was her reply.

"But I know what I shall insist on," said Stuyvesant.   "It is Kitty!"

"Somebody must have told you!" was her laughing confession as she withdrew her hands.

"And this is the reward I claim," said Stuyvesant, as he sprang up and clasped her in his arms and kissed her.

"Don't, Paul," she cried, "don't! You will muss my hair, and I've just been fixing it.   There, that will do."

"Just one more," he pleaded.

"Well, then, just one."

He took two.

"And now," she said, "sit down where I can see you, and behave like a lady, and not like a great, big, rough bear!"

Stuyvesant obeyed her, and took a seat on a sofa; she came and sat down by his side.   Probably no one who might see a photograph of Miss Katharine Vaughn

would call her handsome, but certainly
no one could talk to her half an hour
without declaring her charming.   Her
face was not sufficiently dignified or regular to deserve to be accepted as beautiful, but she had lively eyes, a bright
smile, lovely light golden hair, which
clustered in little curls behind her ears
and around her neck, and she was received as a pretty girl in a city where
there is no lack of pretty girls.   Perhaps
her charm lay rather in her manner than
in her looks—in her expression, in her
variety, in her brilliancy.   But that she
was charming no one who knew her well
would ever dream of denying; that she
was pretty, few would dispute; and that
she was really beautiful, Paul Stuyvesant
believed as he believed in the immortal-
ity of his soul.

"Don't you want to come out for a
walk?" asked Stuyvesant, when the first
fervor of the meeting was over.

"I want to walk, of course," she answered, "but I can't.   I meant to have
told you yesterday evening, but I forgot.
At one o'clock I'm going to a grabiola."

"A what?" he inquired, surprised by this strange vocable.

"A grabiola," she replied, laughing: "that's what I call it. It is a girls' lunch where there are so many of us that we don't sit down, but have to stand around and *grab* our food the best way we can. That's a grabiola. I hate 'em generally; even regular sit-down luncheons are poky enough, goodness knows." And then if you could hear the way some of those girls talk, you would be scared out of your seven senses. Are there seven senses, or five, or three? I always forget," she asked with amusing frankness

" And how can you expect me to remember," he answered gallantly, "when you know that I always lose my senses in your presence?"

"That's not so bad—for a beginning," said the young lady. "Go up head!"

It is to be noted that Miss Katharine Vaughn had caught from her artist brother a certain pictorial vivacity of language which often came perilously close to the verge of slang. But her lover was under

4

the spell, as a lover should be, and he was ready to pick up for a pearl or a ruby whatever might fall from her lips.

"I do wish you could just hear those girls talk," she went on: "sometimes I can't even get in a word edgeways."

"Not even a sharp one?" he inquired, smiling

"Now, that isn't fair, Paul. Indeed, it is really unkind! Have I ever said a sharp word to you?" And she looked at him appealingly.

"My dear Kitty," he hastened to protest, "I didn't mean to insinuate——"

"If you didn't mean it, why did you do it?" she retorted. "That's what Mme. Parlier used to say to us at school. You didn't know me, Paul, when I was in the graduating class at Mme. Parlier's Institute for Young Ladies! French is the language of the school. I used to translate slang into French. Sometimes she really strained herself trying to guess what I meant by saying, '*Eh bien, je sourirais,*' and '*Cela prend le gâteau.*' We did have dead loads of fun sometimes."

"Did Mme. Parlier have dead loads of

fun also?" asked Stuyvesant. "I suppose she was like the frog in the fable: what was fun to you was death to her."

"We didn't kill her. She is as fat and as jolly as ever. I go to see her two or three times a year. She always asks me if we are keeping up our studies. Last time I saw her she asked if I could speak Italian yet, and I answered that I couldn't exactly speak *Italian*, but I could still dance the *German*. I think that puzzled her a little. Now I really must send you away. I have lots to do before I go to lunch. I haven't had a minute to myself all day, and I shan't have. You needn't smile—just as if you men did all the work and we women were mere idlers."

Stuyvesant inquired what it was which had kept her so busy.

"Well, at nine o'clock this morning I had to be at the Industrial School——"

"To learn industry?" he asked hastily.

"To teach poor children how to sew," she answered. "Incidentally they learn *manners* also; and if you would like to take lessons, perhaps you had better apply for admission."

Stuyvesant laughed lightly as she made this quick return.

"And what else have you done to-day?" he asked.

"At half-past ten I went to Mrs. Duncan's, where our Shakespeare Club met. Gladys Tennant and I read two acts of 'As You Like It.'"

"Do you know why you remind me of Rosalind?" he asked.

"I suppose she was good-looking," she replied pertly.

"That's not the reason."

"Then what is it?"

"Because," Stuyvesant answered, "I can say of you what Orlando said of Rosalind. You are 'just as high as my heart.'"

"Really, Paul," she said, rising, "as long as you say pretty things like that I shall hate to turn you out. But I must dress now, or I'm sure to be late. I'll be good to you, though. You can come back for me—let's see: after lunch. I'm going to the New York Hospital. You can come at half-past four and walk there with me."

"What on earth takes you to the hospital?" was Stuyvesant's surprised inquiry.

"You will take me there—if you come for me in time," was her answer.

"I mean, why are you going there?"

"To read to the children. A lot of us girls have agreed to go twice a week, and it's my turn this afternoon. The Bishop of Tuxedo suggested it to us, just before he went West."

"Isn't the Bishop of Tuxedo still here?" Stuyvesant asked, at once recalling her brother's excuse for breaking his next morning's appointment.

"He started on Monday, I think," was her reply.

"And isn't he going to be back soon?"

"Not unless you call three months soon," she answered. "He told us last Sunday he was going on a sort of tour of inspection as far as California."

"Are you certain that he has gone?"

"Yes: one of the girls at the sewing-school this morning said that she had seen him driving down to the ferry. She didn't say whether it was Monday or Tuesday; but it was early in the week."

"And he will not be in town here to-morrow?" Stuyvesant asked the question with the vain hope that perhaps Charley had not deceived him.

"Of course he won't be here to-morrow. Didn't I tell you he was going West, young man, to grow up with the country?"

He did not answer her. It was with a shock that he discovered that Charley Vaughn had invented the reason for breaking the appointment. Under other circumstances, he would not have thought twice about the matter; he would have accepted the artist's elaborate excuse as an ingenious fiction intended merely to hide the real reason. But now, since he had seen the name of James Burt on the back of the check given to Charles Vaughn, Stuyvesant was strangely suspicious. He was in the frame of mind in which a man is ready to twist things innocent enough in themselves into a startling semblance of wrong. He was conscious of this himself, and he tried to throw off the cloak of doubt and distrust which enveloped him.

"Have you seen Charley to-day?" he asked, as Katharine Vaughn came with him to the head of the stairs.

"I've only seen him twice this week," she answered. "And I wish he'd come oftener, for I don't think he's at all bright just now."

So she had noticed it too, thought Stuyvesant.

"I don't know what's the matter with him," she continued. "At first I'd an idea that he might be in love. I didn't like that at all, for of course I had meant to pick out the girl myself that Charley was to marry."

"Do you think that is what's the matter with him?" Stuyvesant asked eagerly, hoping that some simple and natural reason like this might suffice to explain the change in Charley's manner which both his sister and his friend had noticed.

"I don't know," she answered. "Charley in love would be a funny sight, wouldn't it? You might sell tickets at the door, and that alone would be worth the entire price of admission. You know that he is odd enough as it is, in some

ways.   I don't know what to think about
it.   He's always talking about his best
girl and his second-best girl; but he has
never told me who his best girl is.
That's very suspicious, isn't it?"

Stuyvesant asked whether she had noticed that her brother was attentive to any
particular young lady.

" He's attentive to them all, you know:
that's just the trouble," was her reply;
" he's so amusing, they all dote on him.
Perhaps he has been more taken with
Gladys Tennant than any one else; but I
haven't seen them together anywhere
lately, and Gladys never talks about
him.   But do you remember how they
flirted together that night at your theatre-
party?"

Stuyvesant reminded her that he had
met Miss Tennant only once, when she
had been invited by Kitty to the theatre-
party and to the following supper.   Then
he asked her if she thought that her
brother was really interested in the young
lady.

"I don't know," was the reply.   "I
thought he was beginning to take notice;

but I wouldn't bet big money on it—as he would say."

"Is she interested in him?" he asked next.

"I don't know about that, either," she answered. "Of course she's a girl, and doesn't let on how she feels or what she thinks. She's been flirting lately with Jack Dobbin—you know that little Frenchified dude who went to Paris a year or two ago as Johnny Dobbin and came back this fall with an imported accent, now calls himself M. Jacques d'Auban, and says his ancestor drew a long-bow at the battle of Poictiers. When he told me that I wanted to tell him that he was following in the family footsteps—and drawing a long-bow now. But I mustn't stay here chattering to you, or I shall be late at the grabiola."

They were standing at the top of the stairs as she said this, but Stuyvesant seemed in no hurry to descend them.

"Be off with you!" she cried, as she saw that he made no movement to go.

"I'm not in a hurry," he remarked calmly.

"But I am. Where. are you going now?"

"Wherever you wish me to go."

"Then run down to Maiden Lane, and tell them to hurry up that tennis-racket of mine you took to be restrung. We are going to play twice a week during Lent. You can report about it when you come here at half-past four to take me to the hospital. And go at once, or I shall be late at my lunch."

Probably Miss Katharine Vaughn was a little late at that lunch, since it was set for one o'clock, and the factory-whistles were shrilly announcing that hour when Paul Stuyvesant left her house.

CHAPTER V.

MR. PAUL STUYVESANT GOES DOWN-TOWN.

BUT it was half-past one by the broad dial of Trinity Church when Stuyvesant turned into Broadway from Maiden Lane, having attended to Miss Vaughn's commission. He stood for a moment on the corner irresolutely. He had nothing to do and nowhere to go until the time came to call again on her. Having begun the day by oversleeping himself, he had given himself up to laziness; and he knew that he would accomplish little or nothing even if he should summon up energy to return to his apartments, where the incomplete manuscript of "A History of Circumstantial Evidence" lay reproachfully on his desk.

He glanced up and down the busy thoroughfare, from which gangs of swarthy laborers were rapidly removing the snow

now trodden into a dark mire. The sun
shone brightly, and the sharp breeze made
him button his coat and again put on his
sealskin gloves, which he had pocketed
while inquiring about the tennis-racket in
an overheated store. The bracing atmos-
phere invited a walk, and Stuyvesant
turned his footsteps to the Battery, always a favorite loitering-place of his.

And yet, long before he reached the
Battery, Stuyvesant stayed his feet and
turned aside. As he came almost in
front of Trinity Church, he suddenly rec-
ollected that the office of Eliphalet Duncan was in the Bowdoin Building, No.
76 Broadway. Ever since he had seen
Duncan's indorsement after James Burt's
on the check he had given to Charley
Vaughn, Paul had a desire to meet the
lawyer and to ask him—well, he did not
know exactly what it was he wanted to
ask his friend. He could not get Charley
Vaughn out of his mind. Even the im-
age of Kitty, vivid as it was usually,
was obscured by that of her brother.
Who was the M. Zalinski to whom
Charley had given the check ? And what

was his connection with the James Burt whom Duncan was defending for having burglars' tools in his possession?

So it was that when Stuyvesant came in front of the building where Duncan's office was, he entered it; and the elevator soon deposited him opposite the door which bore his friend's name.

But Mr. Duncan was not in, so the clerk told him. Mr. Duncan had returned from a reference a quarter of an hour before, and he had only just gone out to lunch. Would Mr. Stuyvesant wait for him?—he would probably return in a few minutes.

Mr. Stuyvesant would not wait for him, because Mr. Stuyvesant thought he knew where he would find him without waiting.

In one of the small streets, almost under the shadow of Trinity steeple, there is a quaint little old house. It is, indeed, one of the oldest houses in New York; for it was built when New York was yet New Amsterdam. It was once the dwelling of a Dutch burgher transplanted to the New World, where he had sought to reproduce the comfort to which he had been accustomed in his native land. It was now decayed and worn with years; its timbers were rotting at last, and its floors were uneven. It had been patched and braced up and treated with reverent care; but it was a very old house, and its time was soon to be completed.

It was now occupied as a chop-house. Within its dusky parlor, with its heavily cobwebbed ceiling and its cleanly sanded floor, the New Yorker came for his mid-day meal. The fare which could be had there was simple and excellent. A chop off the grill, a baked potato, a kidney, a fresh mushroom, a porterhouse-steak— these were luxuries obtainable at Tom's as they were to be had nowhere else in America. The place was called Tom's. Who Tom was, or rather who he had been, and where he had lived, and where he had gone—these were all questions which the frequenters of Tom's forbore to ask, well knowing that they could get no answer. The present proprietor was a portly Englishman, who had once been an actor. Such at least he was wont to boast himself to a new customer after a

second mug of his own half-and-half.   An
inquisitive reporter had, after a long and
difficult search, succeeded in finding the
playbill of a performance of " The School
for Scandal " at old Wallack's Theatre, on
Broadway, near Broome Street, on which
Mr. Hodges' name appeared as the im-
personator of Lady Sneerwell's servant.
Whatever Mr. Hodges' histrionic faculty
or his theatrical reputation might be, before he " retired to private life to keep a
public-house," no one could dispute the
quality of the refreshment he offered to
his customers; and, in consequence, the
two small rooms which constituted the
ground-floor of the little old house were
always inconveniently crowded from half-
past eleven to half-past two, six days out
of seven.   What became of Tom's on
Sunday, or where Mr. Hodges spent that
day of rest, no man ever thought to ask.

It was here, in the little parlor of
Tom's, that Stuyvesant found his friend,
just about to beign on a kidney fresh
from the gridiron.   At the moment Paul
entered the room the seat opposite to
Eliphalet Duncan's was vacated by a ro-

bust stock-broker, who put on a showy overcoat and strode forth with a stately step which made the little old house shake to its foundations.

Stuyvesant slipped into the vacant seat, saying nothing, and waiting until Duncan should look up. At last the lawyer raised his mug of ale to his mouth, and his eyes were lifted from his plate.

"Paul Stuyvesant!" he cried in surprise. "How the deuce did you get in?"

"Through the door," answered Stuyvesant. "Is thy servant a spook, that he should glide in through the wall or pass up through the floor?"

"Now you are here, and however you got here, have some lunch," said the lawyer.

"I breakfasted late, and I have no appetite; but a kidney like the one on your plate would tempt Lucullus after his banquet."

Stuyvesant did not really want anything to eat. What he sought was an excuse for sitting down with Duncan, in the hope that the course of conversation might so turn that he could twist in an

allusion to James Burt, and thus lead up
to an inquiry as to M. Zalinski.   To ask
outright about either of them would force
him to declare the reason why he wanted
the information; and he was not willing
to mention Charley Vaughn's name carelessly.   He did not choose to confess,
even to himself, how anxious he was to
free his own mind from the strange doubts
which clouded it.

"Do you know anything about pictures?" asked Duncan rather abruptly,
after they had discussed two or three of
the minor topics of the day.

"I refuse to commit myself to a confession of complete ignorance," answered
Stuyvesant.

"Of course," said Duncan.   "But I
doubt if you know much more about them
than I do."

"That depends on how much you
know."

Stuyvesant laughed, and went on to ask
why his friend's thoughts had been turn-
ing-again to art.

"Because of that despatch in the paper
this morning," the lawyer answered,

5

"about the stealing of that picture by Titian. There's a thing I cannot understand."

"What is there so extraordinary about it?" asked Stuyvesant.

"That any one should have stolen it at all, that's what's extraordinary."

"But isn't the picture very valuable?"

"Of course," replied Duncan; "but what good will that do the thief? He can't sell it. Nobody will buy it. Every man in the world who knows that that picture is more valuable than a tea-store chromo knows also this morning that it has been stolen."

"I see," said Stuyvesant. "You mean that the thief cannot profit by his theft."

"That is just what I do mean. He might as well have stolen the Koh-i-noor, for all the good it will do him."

"I should think the stealing of the Koh-i-noor even a safer enterprise and more likely to pay," Stuyvesant returned, "because a big diamond can be broken up, just as silver can be melted down."

"Of course," said Duncan. "And that is what puzzles me. What did any man run the risk of prison to take that which is of no use to him? That floors me, I confess. Problems of criminal psychology have a strange fascination for me, and I like to grapple with them resolutely. I have been turning this one over and over ever since I read the news at breakfast, and I am just as far from a solution as ever."

"This is not the first time a picture has been cut from the frame and carried off," suggested Stuyvesant.

"There have been other instances, I know; but that doesn't help me to an explanation," Duncan rejoined. "Sometimes it has been done from malice, sometimes with the hope of a reward for the return of the stolen goods; and sometimes, I think, the real cause has been some sort of pictorial monomania on the part of the thief."

"A strange madness that would be," Stuyvesant commented.

"Of course," said Duncan; "and yet not so very strange. That a man should be so taken with a picture—so fascinated by it, so overpowered by its beauty—that he should steal it, to have it always at his command, even though he could never show it to any other human eye, that I can understand. I have enough of the artist in me to understand that."

Stuyvesant looked up seriously.

"Do you mean to say," he said, "that you believe that a man might be led to steal a picture simply out of sheer artistic appreciation of its beauties, merely to have it in his possession where he could see it at will, and yet knowing that he could never show it to any one else?"

"That's exactly what I do believe," answered Duncan. "Such things have happened. Such a thing may have happened in this case. Indeed, the longer I think about it, the more inclined I am to believe that this Mary Magdalen of Titian has been stolen by some enthusiastic admirer of Titian's painting——"

"Like Charley Vaughn," said Stuyvesant, smiling at the idea.

"Like Charley Vaughn," repeated Duncan; "and Charley, being an enthusiast about Titian, is likely to be acquainted with others as enthusiastic as he is. Perhaps he could guess who the thief was. If the picture doesn't turn up soon, I'll have a chat with Charley, and maybe we can give the police a clew or two."

"I can see that the motive you suggest is just possible," remarked Stuyvesant, "but it does not seem probable. Your other explanation, that perhaps the picture had been taken to hold for a ransom, strikes me as far more plausible."

"Of course," said Duncan, "it *is* more plausible; but, for all that, I think the other is quite as likely to be the right explanation."

"Is it absolutely impossible for the thief to dispose of a picture as well known as this Titian?" asked Stuyvesant.

"Absolutely impossible," replied Duncan, "or at least I should say so, if I did not know what extraordinary things a receiver of stolen goods is sometimes willing to buy."

As Duncan paused, Stuyvesant wished he knew exactly how to bring in the name about which he wanted to inquire. The conversation was taking just the turn he had hoped for; and he felt that it would be his own fault if he left Tom's without the information he was seeking. Before he could find the words which would do what he wanted, Duncan saved him the trouble.

"We've had for a client lately," said the lawyer, "a notorious old 'fence,' as they call a receiver of stolen goods. I have had to defend him on a charge which the police trumped up against him. No doubt he had been guilty of many other offences, but of the particular offence which they charged against him he was innocent, as it happened. And in the course of my interviews with him, when I was preparing his defence, I got an inside view of his business, and I learned not a few of the tricks of the trade. This Zalinski told me once——"

"Zalinski?" interrupted Stuyvesant. "Michael Zalinski?"

"Yes," replied Duncan; "his name is Michael. But what do you know about him?"

"And he is a receiver of stolen goods?" pursued Stuyvesant.

"A 'fence,' if you prefer the phrase," was the answer.

"Is he an accomplice of James Burt's?" asked Stuyvesant.

"Now, what, in the name of common sense, do you know about James Burt?" was Duncan's astonished demand.

In answer, Stuyvesant took out his pocket-book and drew from it the cancelled check he had given to Charley Vaughn. He showed it to Duncan, and then, turning it over, he drew the lawyer's attention to the indorsements:

Charles Vaughn.

M. Zalinski.

James Burt.

Eliphalet Duncan.

"So that's where you picked up the name, is it? I remember the check well enough," Duncan said. "Burt paid it me as a retainer."

"I surmised as much," Stuyvesant interjected: "they are accomplices, I suppose, Zalinski and Burt—'pals' you call them, I believe?"

"They are close friends, certainly," Duncan answered. "It was Zalinski who persuaded me to take up Burt's case in spite of my distaste for criminal practice."

"And what manner of man is this M. Zalinski?" asked Stuyvesant, conscious of not a little constraint.

"He's an odd fish—a Polish Jew, I think, and not yet wholly Americanized. He has his good points and his bad—like the rest of us. One of his peculiarities is that he keeps no bank-account, although he is making money hand over fist. If he gets a check he pays it out again as soon as he can. That's the way I came to get this check of yours. Charley gave it to Zalinski, and he passed it along to Burt as soon as he could——"

"In full payment for stolen goods, I suppose, and no questions asked?" suggested Stuyvesant.

"Perhaps, and perhaps not," Duncan answered. "He may have lent Burt the money, or even given it to him outright; there's no knowing. The two men are 'thick as thieves in Vallombrosa,' to use a merry jest of Charley's."

"Does Charley know this burglar of yours?" inquired Stuyvesant, with an affectation of levity.

"How should he?" returned Duncan in surprise.

"I thought that he might, perhaps," Stuyvesant explained feebly.

"Of course," Duncan continued, "for all I know, Charley may be an intimate friend of my burglar, as you call him; I can't say. But he has had dealings with Zalinski more than once, I'm sure."

"How do you know that?" asked Stuyvesant, with an increasing sense of dangerous discovery.

"Because Zalinski has twice given me checks drawn to his order by Charley," the lawyer replied.

Stuyvesant looked at him in astonishment.

"Do you mean to say," he managed to inquire at last, "that this check of mine is not the first that has come to you bearing the signatures of both M. Zalinski and Charles Vaughn?"

"I think it's the third," his friend answered; "the other two were Charley's own checks, drawn to Zalinski's order and by him indorsed over to me as part of my fees."

Stuyvesant wanted to ask Duncan if he could suggest any reason why Charley should pay money to a receiver of stolen goods. The question framed itself in his mind, but it stuck in his throat. He could not bring himself to ask it. He was not willing to excite Duncan's suspicion by any untoward inquiry.

He looked up at Duncan with an anxious glance of examination. Although he dared not inquire, he wondered how the lawyer explained to himself the strange conjunction of the artist, the "fence," and the burglar. Stuyvesant himself had no explanation to offer; he was wholly at a loss. He did not know what to think. That his own check given to Charley should have passed into the hands of Zalinski was remarkable enough. That Charley should twice before have paid Zalinski money was even more extraordinary.

Before Stuyvesant could invent a plausible method of pursuing the conversation, and adroitly eliciting Duncan's opinion on the transaction, a single stroke from the steeple of Trinity declared that it was half-past two. The lawyer rapped on the table.

"You must excuse me, Paul," he said, as the waiter came up; "but I have an appointment with a client in a quarter of an hour."

"I must be off myself," returned Stuyvesant, rising as though he were in a hurry, his mental trouble communicating itself to his body.

Duncan paid the waiter, and the two friends wended their way out of Tom's and turned toward Broadway.

In the midst of the crossing and scattering throng it was impossible for Stuyvesant to continue the conversation in the tone he wished for. And yet before they came to a stop at the broad white marble steps of the Bowdoin Building, where Duncan had his office, Stuyvesant had managed to express his curiosity about Zalinski so as to lead the lawyer to tell

him just where the receiver of stolen
goods lived.   It was in Bleecker Street,
about two blocks west of Broadway.

After a few words of hasty farewell,
they shook hands, and Duncan went into
the building before which they were standing.

As soon as his friend had gone, Stuyvesant took out one of his cards and
wrote down the exact number of M. Zalinski's place of business.

CHAPTER VI.

MR. PAUL STUYVESANT CALLS ON M. ZA-
LINSKI.

STUYVESANT had abundant
subject for thought as he
pursued his course northward
along Broadway, walking
briskly to keep his blood in circulation
until a car should overtake him.   Michael
Zalinski was a "fence"—a receiver of
stolen goods—a man of a class which
Paul knew as having an existence in every
great city, in common with the burglar,
the bunco-man, and the lawless element
generally, but with which he had never
come in contact personally.   Of the manners and habits of men of this class he
was as profoundly ignorant as he might
be of the daily life of the ichthyosaurus.
And yet he was going to meet this strange
being, familiar enough in the abstract,
but curiously unfamiliar in the concrete.
He was going to beard this undescribed

lion in his den; and he had the street and
number of the den pencilled on a card in
his pocket.   How this pariah of Bleecker
Street would receive him, what he would
be like, how much or how little a mem-
ber of so secretive a profession would
be disposed to tell, and how much or how
little of his communication would be
worthy of credit, Paul did not know.

It was a singularly distasteful mission,
this on which he was bent.   As an ama-
teur he enjoyed a bit of detective work.
He admired the skill of Gaboriau's detec-
tives, although he recognized that the
problems they encountered were invented
only to be solved.   Probably it was an
unacknowledged taste in this direction
which had led him to adopt the fallacies
of circumstantial evidence as the subject
of his first book.   But this was little
more than a clever man's satisfaction in
the successful piecing together of an ingenious puzzle.   Paul's mind followed
Lecoq willingly enough through slums
and haunts into which Paul himself would
never have dreamed of taking his body.
And yet he was now on his way to the

shop—the house—the lair—how should it be termed?—of a "fence."

The connection of a "fence" with the outside world, so Paul argued, must needs be twofold. The receiver of stolen goods is the manager of the jobbing and commission house of crime. Like other commission houses, it must buy from the producer to sell to the consumer. Therefore he will pay money to the one and receive it from the other. James Burt, the housebreaker, is a producer—that is plain enough; and nothing was more natural than that Zalinski should pay him money —Charley's check, for instance. This reasoning was a sensible relief to Stuyvesant's mind. Of course he did not suspect Charley of anything wrong; he would have scoffed at any one who should have suggested that he might come to believe that the young artist was guilty of any evil; yet it was a relief to remember that because a man pays money to a receiver of stolen goods there is no reason to suppose that he has been selling plunder.

Of course Stuyvesant had read "Oliver Twist," and he had seen the play which

has been made out of it.   Fagin, he as-
sumed, was a tolerably correct portrait
of a typical "fence;" but Fagin belonged
to the London of half a century ago,
while Zalinski belonged to the New York
of to-day.   A change of climate and an advance of forty years or more would naturally make many a modification in Fagin.

These mental queries were idle, he
confessed to himself; for he would soon
know what manner of man Zalinski might
be.   Here was the number.   He stopped
in surprise and doubt, staring hard at the
house in front of him, as though he had
made a mistake.

Opposite him a door swung and creaked
as some one passed out.   Over his head
glittered the arms of Lombardy, and beneath a legend in tarnished gilding set
forth:

M. ZALINSKI,
LICENSED PAWNBROKER.

LIBERAL ADVANCES ON ALL KINDS OF
PERSONAL PROPERTY.

UNREDEEMED PLEDGES FOR SALE.

Stuyvesant had never bargained for this. The "fence" was bad enough; but, in a way, the pawnbroker seemed infinitely worse. Around the one had hung the halo of some sort of mystery; while the other stood boldly confessed as the licensed conductor of a shabby, sordid, and (in Paul's eyes) degraded trade. And Charley had paid this man money—not once, nor twice, but several, perhaps many, times. And Duncan, ignoring the ostensible business altogether, had spoken of him as a "fence."

The door swung back once more, and then hung, quivering and complaining, in its normal position, half open, half shut, as two young men passed out.

One of them was attaching a latch-key to his watch-chain as he came down the steps.

"Time's up," he remarked, with a coarse, reckless laugh.

"And it's likely to be up for a while," responded the other. "D'ye see those three balls?" and he pointed upward "D'ye know what they stand for?"

"Do I?" said the first speaker, some-
6

what bitterly. "I think I've had a good chance to learn."

"They mean that it's two to one you don't' get anything out, once you put it in."

"Double the odds and it's a safe bet still," said the young man, buttoning his coat so as still to display the watch-chain. "Devil may care, for all of me. Come on: we've got the boodle now; let's go somewhere and get a ball for ourselves."

"I'm with you," replied the other, with evident alacrity.

Stuyvesant watched them as they passed down the street, until the nearest saloon swallowed them up. They had not far to go.

He walked away to the next corner and paused there for a moment. He felt an almost invincible repugnance to enter the place. It seemed to him as if he would leave something of his self-respect behind him. What would Kitty think if she were to see him going into a low, disreputable pawnshop or coming out of it? Then he laughed to himself, as he glanced up and down the street; it did not seem a likely promenade for a fashionable young lady.

Stuyvesant was fully conscious that there was nothing wrong or dishonorable in what he was about to do; and yet, if he had been going to commit a theft he could not have felt more nervous and uncomfortable than he did as he ran up the steps and pushed open the creaking door. He let it fall behind him, glad to screen himself from the street, yet feeling more like a sneak than he had ever felt in his life before.

He found himself in a long room which ran the entire depth of the house, the partitions having been removed. It had a close, musty smell, in strong contrast to the keen, frosty air without. Little daylight filtered through the unwashed windows; but the place was bright enough with the garish brilliance of half-a-dozen flaring gas-jets. To the left of the entrance-door the view was obscured by a couple of wooden screens, which served to wall off little spaces not unlike the stalls in a confessional. These were for the transaction of business with such cus-

tomers as might feel a delicacy about ne-
gotiating their loans in the bold public-
ity of the main shop. Paul tried each of
these three sanctuaries in turn, but all
three of them were occupied.

Down the entire length of the room
ran an extremely broad counter of
cheaply-painted wood, stained and dirty,
and worn smooth at the edges by clinging hands. The wall behind it was com-
pletely hidden by a succession of shelves,
filled to their utmost capacity with queer,
nondescript bundles.

"One coat and vest—a dollar ninety!"

Paul turned sharply in the direction of
the strident voice, and saw the whole
long vista of the pawnbroker's shop
stretching out before him in the gas-light,
the package-encumbered wall, the broad
brown counter, the various customers
dotted along it. Poverty's exchange was
doing a rushing business.

A tall and rather good-looking young
man was at the receipt of custom. He
had dark eyes, black, curly hair, and a
shapely, erect figure. As he deftly and
with a practised hand rolled up some

garments into a tight bundle, the glitter of a particularly large, white diamond on one finger caught Paul's eye. Could this be Zalinski? he wondered; and he rather hoped it was.

" Now, don't let the moths get at them," said a frowsy-looking man, who had just —it is to be hoped only temporarily— relinquished possession of the coat and waistcoat.

The young man laughed lightly and pleasantly.

"We can't afford to board no moths here," he answered, as he stepped back and took two small pieces of paper from the clerk at the desk. "You'll find the goods right enough when you come to redeem them—if you ever do," he added in a lower tone, pinning a ticket to the bundle, and adroitly tossing it into a narrow vacant place on the crowded shelves near the ceiling. Then he opened a drawer, slapped a silver dollar, three quarters, and a dime and a nickel loudly on the counter, and pushed them across to the frowsy man along with the other ticket, on which the ink was still wet and shining through the sand that had been sprinkled on it.

"A dollar ninety," he said.   "Next."

"Sure an' that's me," said a trembling voice, and a young woman took her place at the counter.   Paul looked at her with interest.   Under more favorable circumstances he might have thought her a pretty girl, but now, with hollow cheeks and large bright eyes—with a thin, slightly stooped figure, clad for this inclement weather in nothing better than an old calico gown, and a ragged shawl pinned across her shoulders—she seemed pathetic enough.

"Ah, but it's well we're lookin' the day, Mr. Zalinski" (Paul started as he heard the name), "an' as handsome an' fine as iver.   Sure it's a treat for the poor souls that does be comin' here to have the likes of yerself to dale wid."

The young man was evidently not averse from a few compliments.   He caressed his black mustache with the diamond-decked hand, thereby at once displaying the gem and concealing a gratified smile.

"Well, Mary, you give yourself the treat pretty often. What is it to-day?"

"Only a thrifle, sir; it's——" She placed a bundle on the counter, and with nervous fingers fumbled at the knots. Stuyvesant noticed how her hand trembled, and how her dark eyes were raised every moment in mute, despairing appeal to the handsome, self-satisfied face of the young pawnbroker. Her pitiful attempt at humor had died out as the moment for trying her last chance had come.

Zalinski lost patience.

"Come, hurry up," he said roughly. "This isn't a thousand dollar job of yours, I suppose. I can't waste all day over it."

There were tears in her eyes, but she managed to laugh.

"Oh, the sorra a thousand dollars, sir. Sure that's for gintlemen like you, not for the likes of me. I only want——"

She hesitated as the last knot yielded to her hand. She needed so many things that she wanted the last penny she could secure as an advance; but it would be absurd to ask too much, and terrible to

ask too little.   She spread out the con-
tents of the bundle on the counter.

"I want—forty cents on this shawl and
pair of shoes."

The poor shoes were cast back to her
with quick contempt; and, indeed, they
merited no better fate.   Only despair
would have brought them to such a place.

"Call those things shoes!   Take them
to a junk-shop.   Let's see the shawl.
H'm!   I thought so.   I wouldn't take
the whole outfit as a gift.   Forty cents,
indeed!"

"Sure it's better nor this one I have on.
Ye'll let me have a quarter on it, anyhow?"

"What d'ye take this place for?   A
rag-shop?   Take your shawl home and
cut the holes out of it, and then come
back and talk to me."

And then the young pawnbroker turned
away with an indignant sniff.

"Ochone, sir, sure ye'll not be so cruel?
Listen, now!   My man's got a job.   He
goes to work Monday.   Not a word of
lie in it!   Indade he does; and sorra a
thing is there in the house—neither bit
nor sup—and the childer cryin'—an'——"

She tore the thin shawl from her shoulders and added it to the other.

"Won't ye let me have twenty-five on the two? Next week I'll redeem them. They'll be no time wid ye. Ah, look at them ag'in, Mr. Zalinski. Ye'll niver be after refusin' me?"

But the pawnbroker was not even listening to her. He had gone up to one of the more secluded compartments, whence a fairly white hand protruded across the counter. From this hand he had just received a cluster ring, which he was examining in every possible light. No longer did Stuyvesant take comfort from the prepossessing appearance of the man. He was sorry that this was Zalinski.

Meanwhile, the poor Irishwoman had gathered her paltry belongings from the counter slowly and reluctantly. She was weeping unrestrainedly now, and murmuring broken words below her breath.

She did not attempt to make up her bundle again, but placed both shawls over her shoulders; one of them had a gaudy red pattern, and the other was a more sombre black, and—as they were carelessly adjusted, and the colors in the lower one showed through the holes in the upper—the effect was bizarre. She took the shoes in her hand, and turned toward the door.

Paul had never realized the existence of poverty like this. Now and again he had given a trifle to tramps and beggars, always in violation of his principles, for he was a sound theorist in political economy. But here was a genuine case of destitution and despair. He felt a lump rising in his throat as he stepped forward to address the woman.

At this moment the strident tones issued their order to the automaton at the desk:

"Seventy-five dollars on a cluster diamond and ruby ring."

The announcement enchained the attention of every one in the shop. Evidently the transaction was of sensational magnitude.

"What name?" was asked; and from the obscurity of the partition a female voice answered, with a little laugh:

"Cash, Brooklyn."

And the clerk made his entry.

Meanwhile Stuyvesant had found a moment to speak to the Irishwoman. He had not inquired how she happened to be reduced to such a plight; he had not asked what was her husband's business; he had merely slipped into her hand five dollars and his card.

"I am very sorry you are in such trouble," he said. "There is a trifle which may help you along till your husband gets to work. Don't be afraid; I can afford it. And if you'll let me know if there's anything further—if any accident should happen—my address is on that card. I think I know of some people who would inquire into your case, and do more for you than I can."

He turned away from the poor creature's tearful, wondering thanks. Leaving her to marvel what manner of angel this might be who did good in pawnshops, he faced the counter again.

He caught Mr. Zalinski's eye as that worthy returned from depositing the cluster ring in the safe. The young pawnbroker at once accosted Paul, whose dress and appearance suggested another possible transaction of similar importance.

"What can I do for you, sir?" said he politely, half leaning, half reaching across the counter with a suggestive gesture.

Stuyvesant's watch-chain was visible, and from it depended a locket, and in that locket was a very good likeness of Miss Vaughn. The pawnbroker's glance seemed to have been attracted to it, and his hand indicated and in a manner invited it.

Stuyvesant hastily fastened his coat, which he had unbuttoned a moment before to reach his card-case. Having thus answered the gesture in the negative, he proceeded to answer the question in the affirmative.

"If you can spare me a moment, I will tell you. You are Mr. Zalinski, I believe?"

"That is my name," returned the young man, slightly surprised.

As a rule, his customers did not trouble themselves much about his identity, being often more occupied in concealing their own.

"A week or so ago," began Stuyvesant —"just before Christmas, I suppose—you received, doubtless in the course of business, a check——"

He hesitated a moment, uncertain how to proceed; but the young man behind the counter broke in impatiently:

"We receive a great many checks in the course of business. Come to the point at once. I am very busy."

"I am anxious to trace this check. It was drawn by me to the order of a friend of mine, and made payable by him to you. From you it passed to James Burt."

The pawnbroker looked at him sharply and suspiciously.

"You seem to have traced it pretty well already," he said. "I don't know any James Burt. Are you sure the check passed through my hands?"

"It was indorsed M. Zalinski; not a very common name, surely," answered Paul.

"Common or uncommon, it is not

mine. My name is Isaac," was the rough reply.

"Your sign outside reads M. Zalinski," pursued Stuyvesant.

"That's my father's name. This business does not belong to me."

"Can I see your father, then?" asked Paul eagerly.

Somehow, he was relieved to learn that Charley's business did not lie with this shrewd, handsome young fellow, who seemed, like his own diamond, all glitter, without a soft spot anywhere about him.

"Can you see my father?" the clerk repeated slowly. "Well, I don't know; I'll ask him."

He stepped back and took up a speaking-tube which hung at an angle of one of the shelves, and evidently communicated with the regions above. He whistled into it, and held it to his ear waiting for a response. This was not long in coming, for the young man speedily spoke into the tube.

Stuyvesant now listened to a curious, one-sided dialogue: he could hear every word Isaac Zalinski said, but the replies from above were inaudible.

"Gentleman wants to see you a minute," was the first message entrusted to the tube.

Then came a pause. The upper regions were returning their answer.

"I don't know. Something about a check."

Another pause.

"Quite the swell. Talks smooth and dresses well."

The unseen interlocutor apparently took some time to consider this description, and Paul realized that the New York Fagin, behind his open door, was not so accessible after all.

"I don't think so. Never saw him before. Don't look as if he was on any lay," was young Zalinski's next contribution to the interview; and Stuyvesant inferred that the gentleman at the other end had endeavored to connect him with some of the crib-cracking fraternity.

After another application of the tube to his ear, the young man turned:

"Say, young fellow, you're not from Mulberry Street, are you?"

Paul did not for a moment appreciate the significance of the question.

"No: I live uptown," he answered simply.

The other favored him with a protracted stare.

"Well, there's no telling," he muttered to himself, and then sent his voice upward:

Then, after a moment, he dropped the tube.

"The old man'll see you in a minute," he said, and at once returned to the counter, the most eligible point of which was now occupied by an old and portly negro woman.

"Well, Aunt Hannah, what can I do for you to-day?"

There was a bulky bundle in front of the woman. It was neatly pinned up in two towels, which she now proceeded to unfasten.

"Only a trifle, honey," she said. "I hab pressin' occasion fo' a matter ob five dollahs till Monday."

"Gig's coming up then, eh?" said the pawnbroker, with a laugh. "Well, let's have a look at the collat."

"Oh, it's a-comni' this time shuah," said the negress, throwing back the towels. "I dreamed it, I did; an' my ole man, what's never knowed to go wrong, he dreamed it the same as I did."

She took six shirts from the bundle. Paul could see that they were of the finest quality, with initials marked in embroidery, and most beautifully washed and ironed. Zalinski counted them over carelessly and with a disparaging air.

"Give you four dollars," he said at last.

"Foah's no manner ob use to me, honey; must hab five. Couldn't get along with foah, nohow."

"Why, four's enough to gamble away at policy in one week, isn't it? Or has washing taken a boom, that you can afford to plunge this way?" returned the young man.

Paul gasped. This woman was a laundress, and she was actually pawning some of her customers' shirts to risk the money in some obscure form of gambling!

"I tells you, chile, dis yar is shuah! an' I ain't a-gwine to go no little con-

7

temptuous picayune stake on a shuah thing. Not for Hannah!" persisted the old woman.

Zalinski appeared to hesitate a moment; then he cried:

"Five dollars on half a dozen cambric shirts!"

Meanwhile, Paul was plunged in a most unpleasant doubt as to whether his own proper shirts—and he was very particular about his linen—ever passed through an experience like this. He employed a colored washerwoman, and he had never troubled his head to inquire what might be the fate of this personal property from the day he took it off till the day he donned it again. It gave him a cold chill to reflect on the possibility that his shirts might have spent some of the intervening time in such an establishment as this. His laundress lived uptown, it was true, in one of the streets off Sixth Avenue, as well as he could remember; but then there were pawnshops everywhere, and policy-playing was not confined to any particular locality.

A shrill whistle broke the thread of

these unpleasant reflections. He looked up. The sound had come from the tube.

The young pawnbroker was in the act of slapping down five silver dollars and a ticket before the negress. He looked up and caught Stuyvesant's eye; then he nodded.

"That's the old man," he said. "He'll see you now. Go out in the passage and go up one flight of stairs. Room over this, second floor front."

Stuyvesant went out silently; and, following these directions, he soon found himself in front of a closed door at the end of an extremely dark passage. He knocked.

"Come in," said a voice.

As Stuyvesant entered, the sole occupant of the room, who was seated at a desk, spun nimbly round in his revolving chair and faced him:

"Vell, sir, and vot is it I shall haf the bleasure to do mit you?"

The speaker was a man who might be anywhere between fifty and seventy years of age. His thin hair and straggling beard, though streaked with gray, were still dark; and the heavy eyebrows, which came down low over his eyes and nearly met between them, were as black as jet. But his face, as Paul could observe, even in the dim half-light which prevailed, was a perfect network of wrinkles; and a curious twitch which elevated one side of his upper lip at short intervals, after the manner of a snarling dog, whether arising from habit or from infirmity, added a very peculiar character to the man's expression.

By nature and habit, Stuyvesant was a quick observer, and he had seen all that there was to see at a glance. He drew the only remaining chair closer to the desk, and settled himself in it, without waiting for an invitation. It was then that he first noticed the convulsive snarl of the other's lip.

"Mr. Zalinski," he began, "I will not waste more of your time by apologizing for my presence than I am compelled to use. I want to ask you if you know anything of a Mr. Charles Vaughn?"

"I thought it vos apout a sheck you came?"

The old man spoke very rapidly, and with a marked foreign accent, not exactly German, but not unlike it. Paul had some little difficulty in disentangling his meaning from the thick, guttural tones, with their strange inflection and hurried enunciation.

"I am led to make this visit owing to a check of mine which I paid to Mr. Vaughn, and which has returned to me with your indorsement and—and that of others upon it."

"Vós the sheck nicht goot?" asked Zalinski quickly.

"Perfectly good," answered Paul. "It was my own check. I only wished to know, as a matter of curiosity and to satisfy myself, how Charles Vaughn happened to pay it over to you?"

"Hein! and dot vos it all, eh? Und bray vill you dell to me—for guriosity and zatisfaction, as you zay—ish Mr. Sharley Fawn a relative mit you?"

"Not exactly," replied Paul. "At present he is only a friend, but a very dear one, and if he is in any trouble——"

Zalinski's lip twitched upward till it

showed his yellow teeth, as he interrupted:

"Drupple! Vot drupple? Mr. Sharley
Fawn has peesness mit me—peesness,
versteht Sie? Shentlemans who haf peesness mit me don't get into no drupples."

"Not even Mr. James Burt?"

It was so palpable a chance for a hit
that Stuyvesant could not forbear striking, though he regretted his precipitancy
a moment after. Mr. Zalinski's heavy
brows came down, and his mobile lip
went up, till the rest of his face seemed
to vanish between the two, and he was
nothing but snarl and scowl.

"Zee here, young man "—he rose from
his chair and towered over Stuyvesant;
he was an unusually tall man, and the
long-skirted frock-coat that he wore made
him appear even taller—"zee here, young
man, if Shames Purt ish in drupples it
has nicht to do mit me! Nicht! Versteht Sie? Un' if you give shecks to Mr.
Sharley Fawn or Mr. Sharley Anypotty,
you must ogspect that they vill be bad
avay to oder beobles. If you vants to
know vy dot sheck vos to me baid, go un'

ask it of Mr. Sharley Fawn. I don't give avay none of my gustomers' peesness——"

Paul was on his feet too. There was something threatening in the man's tone and manner.

"Mr. Vaughn is a very intimate friend of mine, and I cannot understand how he comes to have business with a person like you at all," he said.

"Hein! He ish, eh? Und you dinks you knows all apout him, eh?"

"I think I do," was Paul's unhesitating answer, though an uncomfortable conviction of the unaccountability of some of Charley's recent proceedings flashed across him as he spoke.

"Vell, I dinks you don't; und if you did, you vos a fool to vaste time goming here to bump me," was the uncompromising reply. "Und I dinks dot I know a goot teal more about Mr. Sharley Fawn as you do—und a goot teal more as I vos a-going to dell you. So!"

"In that case, I have nothing more to detain me here, and I will wish you a good-day," said Paul, turning toward the door.

"Good-tay—good-tay! Und dry und find some peesness for yourself, und maype you will let oder beoble's peesness alone."

And the twitch of Mr. Zalinski's upper lip might have been mistaken for a grin of triumph as he spun round to his desk again, muttering:

"Ikey vos right. No Mulperry Street apout him. He vos no cop; not'ing but a tem fool."

And, though Paul set no special value on Mr. Zalinski's good opinion, the last words of that gentleman rung unpleasantly in his ears as he descended the stairs, and for once in his life he felt strangely inclined to agree with a decidedly unflattering estimate of himself.

CHAPTER VII.

THIS trifling wound to his self-love did not, however, rankle very deeply in Paul Stuyvesant's breast. In the open air, the irritation arising from his unsatisfactory interview with Mr. Michael Zalinski soon evaporated, and he ceased to regard the old man save as a factor in the problem he had undertaken to solve.

Reviewing the situation calmly, Stuyvesant was forced to the conclusion that there had been passages of some kind between the pawnbroker and his future brother-in-law which neither party cared to explain. He wished he had been more explicit with Charley when the latter had called on him that morning; but, after all, at that time he had not been suspicious of anything; at most he had merely been puzzled. Now he was compelled to acknowledge that he had serious misgivings. Duncan, a shrewd, hard-headed lawyer, who had the best possible means of knowing whereof he spoke, had called Zalinski a receiver of stolen goods. The brief conversation Paul had just held with Zalinski had not tended to raise the old man in his estimation. Nor was the transaction that had been brought prominently under his own notice an isolated one. The "fence" evidently knew Charley well; indeed, it seemed to Stuyvesant as though Zalinski had hinted that he knew something of young Vaughn which no one else knew. Of course, this might have arisen from bravado, or from a mere wish to be disagreeable; but, somehow, Stuyvesant feared there was more behind. He had the tangible fact, vouched for by Duncan, that several checks bearing Charley's signature had passed through Zalinski's hands.

Why had this money been paid? Was it hush-money? Did the pawnbroker hold any dark secret as a sword over the young man's head? And before Stuyvesant a vision of that head arose up, always erect, with smiling face and frank honest eyes. With what dark mystery could such a man as Charley Vaughn be mixed up? The thing was melodramatic and impossible.

And yet—and yet—the doubt would obtrude itself. Paul Stuyvesant had read too much and observed too much not to be ready to acknowledge that because a thing is improbable it is by no means impossible, and, indeed, that it is the unlikely which is most constantly occurring. In his own mind he ran over his morning's talk with Charley. The young fellow had been unlike himself; he had been nervous and overwrought; his high spirits had been palpably forced. All this Paul had noticed before the incident of the check had made any but the faintest impression on him. And then the story about the Bishop of Tuxedo! Kitty had told him that the bishop was on his way to San Francisco; so this was a clumsily manufactured excuse. But what, in the name of wonder, had Michael Zalinski to do with it all?

Blackmail was a hideous word, but when once it had occurred to him, Paul could not get it out of his head. If Charley had only confided in him! But then the sufferers from blackmail never confide in anybody. Like the victims of cancer, the slaves of a hideous secret will endure untold miseries to hide their agony as long as possible from even the most sympathetic friends. Paul had studied his Gaboriau closely, and in theory he knew a good deal about blackmailing.

Then his mind ran riot as to the possible nature of the secret hold which Zalinski might have on his friend. He passed in review every crime in the decalogue, and could find none to fit Charley's case with any degree of plausibility. Still, the boy was warm-hearted and impulsive, and would go great lengths to serve a friend. Perhaps the key to the mystery might be found by searching in this direction. Stuyvesant did not attempt to call the roll of Charley's acquaintance: each lived his own life, and each had many friends, unknown to the other even by name. Their circles touched at one point only, and that point was Kitty.

Poor Kitty! How proud she was of her brother, and how she loved him! Paul had once or twice suffered from the wayward temper of his promised bride, and he had solaced himself with the thought that so fond a sister could not but make an affectionate wife. He shuddered at the thought of Kitty's knowing that her brother was in any way entangled with a creature like Zalinski, or of her guessing that he was in the power of such a man. Then and there he registered a vow that he would stand between her and trouble, be the cost to him what it might.

And out of his own mental attitude he fancied he had evolved a clew. Suppose Charley were other than he was; suppose he were a gambler, or a felon, or worse —the degrees of guilt were a little confused in Stuyvesant's mind—would not he (Paul) do anything—pay hush-money, if need be—to keep the knowledge from Kitty? He felt that he would. Thus, having imagined a case in which he himself might be made a ready victim of blackmail, it was easy enough to believe that Charley might have become enmeshed quite as innocently.

Paul pitied the poor boy from the bottom of his heart. He resolved to help him to the uttermost. He would invite his confidence, he would suggest every means that would make the secret easier in telling, and he would pledge himself to an inviolable silence.

He resolved to go straight to Charley's studio. There was a chance of finding him there, and having the matter out with him. Afterward, if there were time, he could keep his appointment with Kitty. Yesterday he could have imagined no duty for which he would have postponed such an engagement; but now he recognized a prior necessity. He did not forego the meeting without a pang, however, and he even looked at his watch, in the hope that he might find time enough for both duty and pleasure. It was only ten minutes past three. He would be able to see Charley, and to meet Kitty afterward. Late as he had gone out that morning, it had been a long day already:

time measures itself less by minutes and seconds than by events and emotions.

He had boarded a Broadway car at Bleecker Street, and, with frequent halts, it was moving uptown. He would get off at Twenty-sixth Street and go across to Charley's studio. So deeply had his mind been occupied that he had to look out to assure himself that he had not already passed that point. He was then just opposite the Star Theatre; and he laughed to himself as he found that he could not recall the circumstance of stepping on the car.

There was a halt at Fourteenth Street, and a great influx of passengers broke into the car by both doors, mostly ladies, homeward-bound from shopping expeditions. The few vacant seats were quickly filled up, and many were left standing. Stuyvesant, always polite, rose and offered his seat to a young lady who was clinging to a strap almost in front of him. With a slight smile and a bow, she sat down, murmuring:

"Thank you, Mr. Stuyvesant."

Paul had all his wits about him in a

moment, and looked down at the young
lady. Before he had finished a few con-
ventional words of disclaimer to her
thanks, he had taken a full mental inven-
tory of her charms, which were neither
few nor slight. She was a tall, graceful
girl, with an exceptionally good figure,
dark brown eyes, a nose a little tip-tilted,
and ripe red lips, around which a couple
of dimples were playing, in pursuit of a
faint smile that vanished as he watched
it. Her most striking feature was her
hair, coiled in magnificent masses over
her shapely head, silken, luxuriant, and
of the color of a withered beech-leaf.
She was certainly a sufficiently remark-
able-looking girl, and to be remembered
when once met; but Paul could not identify her. She seemed to know him; but
who she might be he did not know, and
he could not venture to surmise.

"How inconveniently crowded these
cars always are!" he said, by way of saying something, as he looked down at the
pale, pretty face—far prettier than Miss
Vaughn's, by the way, although Stuyvesant would never have acknowledged that.

Meanwhile, he was saying inwardly: "Now, where on earth have I met that girl? I seem to know her, too; but, for the life of me, I can't find a name or a circumstance to connect her with."

"I suppose the company likes that," she said, answering the remark that met her ears, but leaving Stuyvesant as hopelessly as ever in the dark with regard to the question that was troubling his mind.

"I suppose so," he said, awkwardly enough; and then there was a pause which the conductor, pursuing fares under difficulties, enlivened by treading squarely on Stuyvesant's foot.

"Have you been in New York ever since?" inquired the young lady, when this incident was concluded. "I haven't seen you."

Paul did not quite know how to answer. So far as he knew, the uncertain interval alluded to as "ever since" might have been measured by years or by hours. However, he had to say something.

"Oh, yes, ever since," he answered feebly.

There are few of the minor embarrass-

8

ments of life at all comparable with that of being unexpectedly addressed by some one who knows you, but whom you do not know and whom you are fully conscious you ought to know; nor are the difficulties of the position lessened when the person in question is a young and pretty girl.

"If I was sure I had not seen her for years," thought Paul, "I could remark how much she is grown, for I don't believe she can be twenty; but, as I may have met her last week, I can't risk that."

But a happy inspiration arose out of the reflection.

"How well you are looking!"

"Thank you.   So every one tells me. Kitty Vaughn says——   Oh, by the way, have you seen Kitty lately?"

"I see Miss Vaughn almost every day," answered Stuyvesant somewhat stiffly, not altogether pleased that this fair incognita chose to thread the mazes of his most sacred emotions unrecognized.

"Of course you do; how stupid of me! Well, give her my love, please, and tell her I think it's real mean of her never to come to see me, often as she has promised."

"Perhaps she has forgotten your address," hazarded Paul. If he could pin this unsubstantial acquaintance down to some definite locality, perhaps he might find a name for her. But he was baffled.

"Nonsense! that's altogether too thin! She has my address right enough; but she's afraid of half an hour on the train— that's all that keeps her away."

So the young lady without a name lived outside New York—half an hour by train.

Paul was not much wiser. The locality thus vaguely indicated might be any one of a dozen sylvan retreats in New Jersey or on Long Island; or it might be on one of the several roads running out of the Grand Central station.

"You won't forget? You'll be sure to tell her?" pursued the young lady.

"I won't forget," answered Paul, pledging himself to the possible as embodied in the first part of her sentence, and ignoring the impossible as embodied in the last.

"Are you going uptown?" he asked, when the conversation had languished so long that the pause began to be awkward.

"As far as Forty-second Street, of course," she answered, opening her brown eyes. "I've spent all my money, and now I'm going home again, as a good little girl should do."

Paul laughed a little, as in duty bound.

Suddenly the young lady spoke again, with a quickness that seemed bred of apprehension:

"You're not going to the depot, surely?"

He laughed again, this time with genuine amusement at her evident disquietude.

"No, I am not," he said. "Were you afraid I was?"

She colored a little.

"How absurd! Of course not; but— I—it seemed such an odd time for a gentleman to be going out of town."

"Do you think so?" he answered. "Any day is a good day for that, if there is a stronger attraction in the country than in the city—which is not my case."

She looked at him curiously. He began to congratulate himself on having a little puzzled this girl, who had puzzled him so much. He went on:

"I am only going as far as Twenty-sixth Street, and we're almost there. I am going to call on a Mr. Vaughn, the brother of the Miss Vaughn we were speaking of."

"Are you going to his studio?" she asked, with a quick anxiety which mystified Paul more than ever. This unaccountable girl knew Charley too.

"Certainly, to his studio," he answered. "He is an artist, you know."

"Of course I know that!" she replied, somewhat impatiently. "But are you going by appointment—or—I mean, does he expect you?"

"Not that I know of," answered Stuyvesant, more mystified than ever. "I am just going to drop in on chance. Why do you ask?"

"Oh, nothing," she replied inconsequently, but with an obvious look of relief; and then a mischievous smile set the dimples playing again round the corners of her mouth.

"Of all the riddles!" thought Paul; "but I haven't time to solve it. Here's Twenty-sixth Street."—"I'll say good-by," he added aloud, "and I hope you won't find your half-hour in the train tedious."

"Oh, I'm sure I shan't," she said, with a bright laugh, at the same time frankly extending her hand; "and if you find Mr. Vaughn at home, I hope you will have an immensely pleasant call."

And her merriment, as she spoke, took on a mischievous tone.

Paul raised his hat and left the car.

"Confound the girl!" he thought, "she's laughing at me, and I can't blame her for it; but she was really scared when she began to believe that I was going to the station. If I had nothing better to do, I'd go there just for spite."

But Stuyvesant had something better to do. The temporary diversion afforded by this chance meeting soon faded out of his thoughts when he turned eastward and walked rapidly toward "The Rubens," as the building was called in which Charley Vaughn had his studio.

CHAPTER VIII.

MR. PAUL STUYVESANT INVADES "THE RUBENS."

IN "The Rubens" one studio resembles another, and to describe one is to describe all. It is a room of about twenty feet square. Opposite the door is the broad window which helps to give the exterior of the building its architectural peculiarity. Opposite the window is a gallery eight or nine feet wide, with a balustrade which makes it look like a balcony. Sometimes the gallery is a dressing-room for the model, and a storehouse of odds and ends of one kind or another, studio-properties, lay-figures, studies, sketches, broken frames, and what not, in a disorder problematically picturesque and indubitably dirty.

Paul mounted the stairs: he was an accustomed visitor, and had long since ceased to grumble at the ascent. Following the mute invitation of a painted hand, he knocked at Charley's door. It was opened by a man of about fifty—a man with the typical face of the comic caricature of Irishmen, but preternaturally grave. This face was acidulated by a certain droop of the corners of the mouth and a general twist of the features into an almost vindictive expression of sourness.

"Well, Barney, how are you?"

The old man was a recognized character all over the studio-building, and Stuyvesant knew him well as Charley's particular retainer.

"Bad, sor. What wid the lumbago in the small o' me back, and the rheumatics in me left shoulder, sorra wink o' sleep do I get night nor day."

"That's very bad, Barney," answered Paul, too well acquainted with the old fellow's habitual querulousness to humor it by further sympathy. "Is Mr. Vaughn in?"

"Indade an' I might have known that it wasn't to ax after my health ye've come trapezin' up all them stairs," Barney replied with an injured air.

"You certainly might," said Paul, hardly able to repress a smile at the discontented look on the face of the old Irishman. "I came to see Mr. Vaughn. Is he in?"

"Indade an' he's not," began Barney. By this time Stuyvesant had passed him and entered the studio. "Oh, that's right. Make a liar o' me! What's the good of yer axin' me questions, if ye're not goin' to believe me whin I tell ye?" expostulated Barney, following him into the room. "But sarch, sarch, an' welcome. Sure there's the table he might be under—to say nothin' of the gallery, that 'ud hide a dozen like him. Sarch, if ye want to. Don't be afeared of hurtin' my feelin's; sure I'm used to it."

"I don't doubt you at all, Barney; but I am very anxious to see Mr. Vaughn, and, as I have a few minutes to spare, I'll wait, on the chance of his coming in."

And Stuyvesant pushed a richly-embroidered robe from the most comfortable chair in the room, and sat down.

Barney picked up the mass of drapery and grumbled back with it to the recess under the gallery.

"That's right," he said; "make hay over the whole place. Divil a thing have I to do but to follow the likes of ye round an' clean up yer messes, wid the lumbago in the small o' me back."

"Do you think he'll be in soon?" called Paul, when the muttering began to subside.

"Arrah, what time have I to think, whin me heart's broke wid work? Maybe he will an' maybe he won't; an' that's the nearest I can come to it, for there's no dipindence out of what he says at all, at all."

"And what did he say?" demanded Stuyvesant impatiently.

He knew that the old man was a good servant, honest, faithful, and industrious, and that his one fault was a cross-grained temper, and yet he had often wondered how Charley had endured him so long.

"What did he say, is it?" said Barney. "Well, I'll tell ye that; an' if ye believe him, ye've a better chance of heaven nor I have, if faith'll save ye."

Paul looked at the old man in surprise.

"Don't you think he was telling the truth?"

"I don't think any man's tellin' the truth until I see it proved; an' thin I doubt it," was the uncompromising rejoinder.

"Faith will never save *you*, Barney; that's a fact," laughed Paul. "Now tell me, without any more beating about the bush, when Mr. Vaughn expected to return."

"He *said* he'd be back to-night."

"To-night! What did he mean by that?" Paul inquired at once.

The utter unreasonableness of expecting him to attach a meaning to any man's words was plainly set forth on Barney's expressive features; but he contented himself with a grunt. Stuyvesant saw the futility of expecting help from that quarter; and so, without waiting for a definite reply, he continued:

-"It is very provoking. I wanted to see him particularly, and——By Jove! it's a quarter before four now," he added, glancing at his watch.

"Want'll be yer master, I'm thinkin'," muttered Barney below his breath. "Well, I'm goin' home," he added aloud; "there's no call for me to be waitin' here till dark. If he comes he comes, an' if he don't come he stays away, an' that's all there is to it."

"Does Mr. Vaughn spend much of his time here now?" asked Paul, partly impelled by the wish to say something, and partly on the alert to gain any possible information which might have a bearing on the mysterious business that had taken him there.

Barney was putting on his overcoat, and enveloping his neck in many folds of a long knitted comforter, which somehow had the effect of accentuating his native ugliness to an almost incredible degree.

"No!" he answered, with an inflection of supreme contempt. "He never does be here. He's always off gallivantin'."

The old man moved toward the door, and stopped with his hand on the latch.

"If Mr. Charley comes in while ye're waitin'—which he won't—will ye show him thim letters an' things on the table

forninst ye? They came this mornin',"
he said.

He turned the handle and hobbled out
on the landing, his querulous voice con-
tinuing awhile, till it was abruptly cut
off by the closing of the door.

So Charley spent little time in his
studio, thought Stuyvesant. His work
would seem to have lost its charm for
him, who was once, as Paul well remembered, earnest, eager, and enthusiastic:
all this had changed with the other
changes that had come upon him. His
appetite was poor, too—so Stuyvesant
had gathered from a remark of Barney's;
and a trouble or preoccupation which
will affect the appetite of a man of Charley's age must be serious indeed. Stuyvesant set himself to think: occupied as
he had been lately with Kitty, he had
seen less of her brother. What the date
was when these alterations in his friend
had first begun to force themselves on his
notice, Stuyvesant could not say. It was
only this very morning that something
tangible had brought the matter prominently before him. He was conscious,

now that he looked back, of a hundred trifles, unnoticed at the time, which seemed to indicate a degree of preoccupation in the young artist.

He stopped before the table on which lay the two or three letters and postal-card to which Barney had drawn his attention before going out. His eye fell on them mechanically. He started back with an exclamation, and raised his arm with the gesture with which a man deprecates or seeks to ward off an impending blow.

Exactly on the top of the little pile of mail-matter lay a postal-card, with the address downward. The face of the card, containing less than two lines, written in a bold mercantile hand, lay directly under the eyes of the visitor. Stuyvesant was not conscious of reading these two lines, but unwittingly he had mastered their meaning at a glance. It was as though the words leaped out at him from the paper, and struck him with a force purely physical.

These were the words on the postal-card:

"*Look in and see me at your earliest con-
venience.   M. Zalinski.*"

Stuyvesant fairly staggered.   It seemed
to him as though proof was accumulating
on proof.   This was the embodiment of
the hideous shadow that was darkening
over Charley's life.   There was the hate-
ful name again; and at every step he took
he found it always linked with that of
Vaughn; and Vaughn was Kitty's name,
too.

He took up the card.   It had nothing
more to tell.   On the back were Charley's
name and address; on the face was the
line that had already burned itself into
Paul's brain.   It had done its mission;
it had dealt its crushing blow; and it now
relapsed into seeming insignificance—a
common, every-day postal-card.

The postmark told him it had been
mailed that morning.   Therefore, when
Zalinski had refused to tell him anything
about Charley or their relations to each
other, he had already written to compel
his attendance at that den in Bleecker
Street.   To compel? Yes, to compel;

for, though the note was politely worded, in Paul's eyes it breathed all the authority of an imperious mandate.

There came a sharp knock at the door.

Paul started, almost guiltily, and dropped the card among the other letters. This action, like his action in reading it, was purely mechanical. Indeed, he was so abstracted that it required a repetition of the summons to enable him to recall his wandering thoughts and bid the visitor to enter.

A young fellow, not more than sixteen or seventeen years of age, opened the door and came in. His face was preternaturally sharp, and he had black eyes and a swarthy complexion. He was shabbily dressed; but his clothing was by no means ragged or poverty-stricken. His long overcoat, though shiny with wear and faded into two or three different colors, was a comfortable and seasonable garment enough for the winter. He wore an imitation sealskin cap, which he pulled off as he entered.

" Beg pardon, bister," he began, speaking as if he were suffering from a bad cold

in the head, "was you down to Bister
Zalinski's to-day?"

Zalinski again!   Was he about to learn
something at last?   As this hope flashed
into his heart, Stuyvesant was obliged to
remain silent a moment before he could
command his voice to reply.

"Yes; I was there this afternoon."

"That's all right, then," said the boy;
"'cos he expected you, and bade sure you
would cub sub tide to-day.   He told you
about the frabes, I suppose?"

"He told me nothing at all," Paul answered.   "I couldn't get any satisfaction
from him."

"That's odd, too," said the other;
"'cos he wanted you particular to look
in, and wrote you on purpose."

Paul perceived that the boy took him
for Charley Vaughn, of whose appearance
he was seemingly ignorant.   Should he
undeceive the messenger?   It did not
take him the tenth part of a second to
make up his mind in the negative.   In
Charley's own interests, Stuyvesant would
learn what he could.

These reflections passed through his

9

mind like lightning; and, though the boy continued his sentence with scarcely a perceptible break, he had already decided.

"However," proceeded the messenger, "vot he told me to tell you was this. He has two frabes he'd like you to look at, both forty by twenty-four. One's bodern, but very handsob; and t'other's the regular antique."

"All right," said Paul, and as he was speaking he was trying to think more quickly than he had ever thought in his life before. Was it possible that Charley's visits to Bleecker Street were only in search of cheap picture-frames? Did Zalinski deal in such articles? That was likely enough. Pawnbrokers, so he had heard, sold anything and everything. If this were the innocent explanation of all the strange circumstances, he had acted in his suspicion most unwarrantably. What right had he to question Zalinski, and how could he justify to himself his present assumption of Charley's identity?

But there were more suspicious circumstances in the background still unaccounted for, as he knew, and he felt that he must not jump at conclusions too hastily.

"That's the dibensions you gabe, isn't it?" the boy queried, producing a scrap of paper from his pocket.

Paul took it from him.

"All right, then," the boy continued. "Bister Zalinski has two you can see any time you call. They're just the size for you. Either of them will do for the Bary Bagdalen."

And before Paul could ask another question the messenger of Zalinski was gone.

CHAPTER IX.

MR. PAUL STUYVESANT MAKES A DISCOVERY.

STUYVESANT was left alone with a fresh dread at his heart. "Handsome frame; 40x24; to suit an old master," he read. He simply nodded. His thoughts were too busy. He could not find words. He was conscious of a sudden fear so portentous, so fraught with terrible possibilities, so inexpressibly hideous, that he shrank from analyzing it.

The Mary Magdalen was the great picture, the theft of which had come to light only the previous day. And the shadowy, unexplained connection between two such dissimilar people as Zalinski and Paul's future brother-in-law took shape and substance over a common point—the missing picture!

Stuyvesant was fairly stunned. All

that he had feared, all that his most gloomy previsions had hinted at, was as nothing to this.

" Poor Kitty!" he murmured. A vague, boundless pity for the woman he loved filled his mind. In fancy he saw the sunny head bowed down, the frank, fearless eyes abashed to the earth, in the shadow of her brother's shame. He dared not let his thoughts stray farther in this direction. If ever he needed a clear brain to plan, a steady hand to act, he needed them now; and the vision of Kitty he had conjured up unmanned him.

The Mary Magdalen! The whole story of its curious adventures, its loss and its recovery, as it had been recounted in the newspapers of the day—partly authentic, partly hypothetical—came back to him. And Charley had been one of the first to light upon it in the shop of an obscure Paris picture-dealer. The young painter had discussed the discovery of the picture with him that very morning. He had asked Charley when he had seen the picture last, and the question had remained unanswered. Stuyvesant remembered too

how ardent a longing the boy had ex-
pressed to be the owner of the painting.
Could it be, as Duncan had said, that a
man of artistic temperament might covet
a masterpiece to such a degree that he
would steal it, though he could never reap
any satisfaction from his crime other than
a guilty enjoyment by stealth?   He rec-
ollected that at the news of the theft
Charley had not shown the indignation
which he had expected.   The artist had
contented himself, as far as Paul's recollection served, with a slight expression
of surprise that it had not been found out
before.

And Charley had a Mary Magdalen
in his possession! Zalinski's messenger
had said as much.   Of course, there were
many Mary Magdalens in existence; but
here were the dimensions of the frame,
pencilled in Charley's own writing.
There was a copy of the *Gotham Gazette*
upon the table.   Evidently Charley had
not taken time to open the paper before
going out that morning.   Stuyvesant
hastily unfolded the sheet, and compared
the cabled figures which gave the pict-

ure's dimensions with the memorandum in his hand. They were identical. The measurement of the missing Titian was forty inches by twenty-four.

Although doubt seemed no longer possible, Paul still hoped against hope. He asked himself what opportunity Charley had had to take the picture. Two months and more had elapsed since the artist's return from Paris. The comparison of dates was of little value here, since Mr. Sargent had been absent from Paris nearly seven months, and the picture had not been missed until his return. Any day or any night during seven months might have been the day or night when the picture was cut from its frame. Charley had been in Paris, during Sam Sargent's absence, for nearly three months.

But it was absurd to believe that the boy could have accomplished such a feat alone and unassisted. Stay! Was it so absurd? Charley had admitted, or he had dropped hints that amounted to an admission, that he had seen the Mary Magdalen since its owner had seen it; he had remarked that locked-up apartments were not impregnable, or words to that effect.   Paul remembered this part of the conversation but vaguely.   In any case it was not necessary to assume that the young man had acted alone.   There was a factor in the case which Paul never forgot for an instant.   There was M. Zalinski.

This man was "notoriously crooked," so Duncan had told him.   He was a receiver of stolen goods; quite likely he was in communication with thieves in all the capitals of the world.   Stuyvesant had no idea of the possible ramifications of a business like Zalinski's, but he thought it probable they were extensive.   If the Jew had any part in the removal of the picture, or if he had any knowledge of its removal, there was at once an easy and a terrible explanation of the hold he had over the artist—blackmail!

So Stuyvesant's suspicions had not misled him, after all!   If the old "fence" were in possession of any such secret about a young man in Vaughn's position, he was assured of a revenue to be measured only by the latter's fortune and possible professional earnings. As it happened, the check which Paul had given to Charley, and which had been passed over to Zalinski—the check which had first started him on the trail of this hideous secret—was for a very small sum. But it had not been an isolated transaction. Duncan had spoken of two other checks bearing Vaughn's signature which had reached him from the "fence;" Stuyvesant had not thought to inquire as to their amount, but that mattered little. If three of Charley's checks had been paid by Zalinski to Duncan, dozens might have passed through the same hands into other channels.

But to think that a young man of such position and surroundings, to think that Kitty's brother could ever be guilty of such a crime as robbery, was almost impossible. Perhaps, though he had always been inclined to scoff at the plea, there might be reason to suggest kleptomania. If Charley stole that picture, he must be mad—if ever a man was.

If he stole it? Logically, the doubt seemed hardly tenable; and yet Paul clung to it. In the course of his reading in preparation for his great work, he had seen many an apparently perfect case, perfect in the chain of circumstances that constituted the evidence, fall to pieces under the stronger light of direct proof. Perhaps this case would so crumble away. Perhaps Charley could explain all these seemingly inexplicable circumstances.

If he could but see him!

He paced nervously to and fro. Perhaps Charley would not come; certainly he would not come till late. Through the mist of his general surliness, Barney's opinion on that point had stood out in bold relief, and Stuyvesant was inclined to agree with him. At any rate, if he stayed here any longer alone he felt as if he should go mad himself. He glanced at his watch. He was still in time to keep his appointment with Kitty. He would go.

Under the flaring gas-jet which lighted the room now that night was settling down on the city, there was a table where Charley kept pen and ink and paper.

Stuyvesant set his chair down before this, and wrote a note hastily.   Then he read it over:

"DEAR CHARLEY: I want to see you particularly.   I have waited for you here as long as I can.   I am going out now, but shall be back in my rooms by six o'clock.   Come over there at once when you get back.   I shall not stir till I have seen you, so you can be sure of finding me in.   Don't fail; this is most important.

"Yours,
"PAUL STUYVESANT.
"January 3d, 4:15 P.M."

He placed the note conspicuously on the table, where it would not fail to catch the eye of any one entering the room. Then he turned to go.

Suddenly a thought struck him.   Supposing Charley to be the guilty possessor of the picture, where would he keep it? It was a thing to be guarded jealously from any mortal eye, and nowhere else could the young artist reckon on the same privacy as he could in his own studio.

Of course, it might be at Zalinski's, but the idea that the young fellow would steal the picture to sell again was not to be entertained for a moment. No, if he had it at all, he would keep it somewhere at hand, so that he could look at it occasionally, and take such enjoyment of his surreptitious treasure as his conscience would permit him.

The gallery seemed the most promising place of concealment, and Paul accordingly mounted the steps. One end was curtained off to serve as a model's dressing-room; but a glance behind the hangings showed Paul that it contained nothing in the least resembling what he sought. A pile of dusty canvases occupied one corner. Paul turned them over one by one. They were some of Charley's earlier and cruder efforts—the sketches he had done before he had gone abroad, stored during his absence, and taken back, among other furniture and litter, when he returned and rented this studio. Stuyvesant remembered most of them well, and smiled sadly as he thought of the boyish triumph with which Charley used to refute the uninformed criticisms which Paul had offered, reluctantly enough, and under strong pressure from the artist.

There was nothing to detain him there, and he descended.

This time he went under the gallery, and examined the various hangings that concealed Charley's finished and unsold works. As he raised the curtain which hid the corner farthest from the door, the gaslight fell upon a painting from which he reeled back with a cry of actual pain. Hope itself could go no farther in the face of such a proof. Before his eyes leaned the lost picture—Titian's Mary Magdalen in all the glory of its matchless beauty!

The canvas was nailed to a stretcher; it was unframed, and the ragged edges bore plain marks of the hasty knife of the spoiler. Paul was no art-critic—he was not even a connoisseur; but he could not doubt the genuineness of the picture before him. It had the rich, mellow tone

which the years give to colors; it had all
the breadth and style of Titian's best
work; even Stuyvesant's unpractised eye
could detect and recognize the ear-marks
which had been discussed and insisted
upon by the experts in the various jour-
nals while the authenticity of the Mary
Magdalen had been still a matter of de-
bate.

Stuyvesant dropped the hangings and
came back into the main part of the
studio.   He sank into a chair and asked
himself what he had best do.   To what
purpose would he see Vaughn now?   To
reproach him? to concert measures of
safety with him?   He did not know.   He
took up the note he had written, and was
about to tear it up; but on second thought
he laid it down again.   It would be better to see the boy, better to hear what
he had to say for himself, better to help
him out of this scrape if help were to be
had under heaven.   Charley was Kitty's
brother, and, for Kitty's sake, Paul would
stick to him still.   For her sake, he
would go even to the length of compounding a felony.

Zalinski must be seen and settled with somehow: on that point, at least, Charley could advise him. Then the picture must be returned to the owner if possible. Then arrangements must be made for sending the young fellow away at once—to Europe—somewhere, anywhere—where Kitty should never see him again.

As for himself, he never faltered in his devotion. He thought—and afterward he smiled to himself at the quizzicality of the conceit at such a moment—he thought that if Kitty had ten brothers, each of whom had severally and collectively broken the ten commandments, it could make no difference to him. She was all his world, all his hope, all his future; and his fidelity to her never wavered.

Then he rose and turned down the gas.

It is strange how a methodical man will continue to observe his ordinary habits even when the hopes and ambitions of his life are crashing in ruins around him. He drew on his gloves, and took up his hat and passed out into the hall.

The door, which fastened with a spring-lock, clicked behind him.   He felt as he remembered to have felt the day he returned from his mother's funeral.   The association of ideas was not inapt; for it seemed to him that he was now, as he had been then, turning his back on the place where the dearest friendship of his life lay buried.

CHAPTER X

MR. PAUL STUYVESANT IS LATE FOR AN APPOINTMENT.

S Paul Stuyvesant left "The Rubens," a single stroke from a neighboring steeple told him that he would surely be late in keeping his appointment with Katharine Vaughn. It was at half-past four that she had asked him to call for her to take her to the New York Hospital. By rapid walking he would not keep her waiting more than five or ten minutes. He knew that her imperious character would not brook his apparent neglect to obey her behest.

There was a chill in the air, and a bitter wind swept across the city from river to river. Stuyvesant quickened his pace.

At last he stood before Mrs. Vaughn's door; and then, for all he had hurried, he hesitated. He did not know how to face Kitty or what to say to her.

While he paused in embarrassment and doubt, with his hand extended to pull the bell, the door opened, and Kitty stood before him.

"So there you are!" she cried. "At last!"

"Am I late?" he asked, not knowing what else to say, and glad almost to be scolded if the reproof would keep his thoughts from turning again to the dreadful discovery he had made.

"Late?" she returned. "Well, I should smile—if I wasn't too angry with you ever to smile on you again."

"I hope not," he replied mechanically.

"You were so late that I had given you up, and I was going without you," said Kitty, as she closed the door of her house and started down the steps.

Ordinarily there was nothing that Stuyvesant would have enjoyed more than this brisk walk through the gathering dusk of a winter day with the woman he loved. Even her scolding was as music in his ears generally; and to him it mattered little what she said, so long as he might listen to her voice. But now the music was all discord, and he had no heart for the airy talk about trifles which was wont to give him the greatest delight.

He tried to hide his perturbation from her; but she soon saw that he was not as bright or as lively as usual.

"How came you to forget your appointment with me?" she asked.

"I did not forget it; I was detained."

"That's no excuse at all. You should not let anybody detain you," Kitty returned. "Now, who was she?"

"Who was who?" asked Stuyvesant in surprise.

"Who was the pretty girl who detained you?" she protested.

"But it wasn't a pretty girl who detained me," Paul explained. "It was——"

He checked himself. He could not tell her how or why or where he had been detained.

"Well?" she asked.

Then he saw an opening for a diversion of her attack.

"I was detained by some unexpected

business; but I did meet a pretty girl to-day——"

"Oh!" said Kitty.

Sometimes a monosyllabic interjection may be fraught with a volume of meaning.

"And I wish you could tell me who she is," continued Stuyvesant innocently.

"Do you mean to say that you talk to pretty girls without knowing who they are?" asked she sharply.

"She spoke to me," Paul began to explain.

"Then I am to understand that you let pretty girls whom you don't know speak to you?"

And there was a certain acerbity in the tone of Miss Vaughn's voice as she said this.

"I will tell you the whole story," Stuyvesant answered, glad enough to find a topic about which he could talk without danger.

"Perhaps it would be best," she replied icily.

"I was riding up in a Broadway car this afternoon, when a very pretty girl got on, and of course I gave her my seat," began Paul.

"Would you have given it to her if she had been an ugly old washerwoman with a basket?" interrupted Kitty.

"I hope I should have done so," answered Stuyvesant.

"I have my doubts about it," Kitty returned. "But go on. Your story interests me strangely, as they say in plays. You gave her your seat—and what happened then?"

"She thanked me, calling me by name."

"So then she knew you?" asked Kitty.

"So it seems," he answered.

"And you don't know her?"

"No," he replied; "at least, I have no recollection of having seen her before. Perhaps I may have met her somewhere at dinner or at a reception, but I cannot recall it."

"Oh!" said Kitty again; and Stuyvesant was again conscious of a fall in the temperature.

"What puzzled me most," he continued, "was that she seemed to know that we were engaged.   In fact, she sent her love to you."

"How was she dressed?" asked Kitty.

"I don't know——" began Stuyvesant.

"Of course not.   You are a man," she returned, with a commiserating glance. "What was she like?"

"She was a pretty girl——"

But Kitty interrupted imperiously:

"You have already said that.   What I want to know is, what sort of a pretty girl was she.   Tell me all you happen to have noticed?   I want the truth, the whole truth, and nothing but the truth."

Thus admonished, Stuyvesant described the lady as best he could, and he went over his conversation with her as far as he recalled it.

"A red-headed girl, who lives half an hour out of town.   Of course it was Gladys Tennant," cried Kitty, when he had told his tale.

"Gladys   Tennant?"   he   repeated vaguely.

"Yes," she replied; "don't you remember?   She lives in Yonkers.   I asked you to invite her to that theatre-party;

and at supper she and Charley got up a grand flirtation."

"I think I do recall her now," said Stuyvesant. "And so she and Charley flirted—yes, I remember that too. Let us hope she is not interested in him," he added involuntarily.

"Why?" asked Kitty sharply.

Paul saw his blunder, but it was too late.

"I don't know," he said feebly.

"Don't you think the girl will be lucky who gets Charley?" she continued.

Stuyvesant could not forget the facts he had just found out. He could not thrust out of his mind the strange secret he had discovered in her brother's studio. And before he could make ready an answer, she went on:

"Don't you think Charley is good enough for any girl?"

"Yes," replied Stuyvesant hastily, knowing how dear brother and sister were to each other—"oh, yes! I have always said that Charley was a good fellow."

"That's what you say about him, is

it?" asked Charley's sister. "And that's how you say it?"

"I shall always stand up for him," went on the unlucky Paul. "I hope he will always find a friend in me."

Kitty withdrew her hand from Stuyvesant's arm.

"I see that you have some grievance against Charley," she said coldly. "But I think it would be more manly of you to go to him and have it out than to make insinuations to me!"

"Kitty!" cried Paul, astonished at this outbreak.

"I have known Charley longer than I have known you," she continued, "and I know him better than you do."

"I do not doubt it," he returned; "but——"

He checked himself again. What could he say? There was nothing to do but to bear her reproaches in silence. He could not justify himself. He could not tell her what he knew about her brother; he could not tell her that for her sake he stood ready to do anything in his power for Charley, if he might yet save the unfortunate and misguided boy.

And so it was that they walked on in silence, side by side, down Fifth Avenue to Fifteenth Street.

They turned the corner, and in less than a minute they stood before the broad portal of the New York Hospital.

"Here is where I am going," said Miss Vaughn icily. "I will not trouble you any further, Mr. Stuyvesant."

Paul started as she addressed him thus formally, and he gave her a reproachful glance.

"It is never a trouble to do anything for you," he returned. "It is always a pleasure to be with you."

Miss Vaughn had left him without shaking hands, and she mounted the few steps before the door. Then she turned: perhaps she had caught his reproachful glance; perhaps the sorrowful tones in his voice touched her; at any rate, she relented a little.

Standing on the steps above him, she looked down and said:

"I shall be here until a quarter-past

six.   You may come back for me then, if you like."

Before Stuyvesant could speak, he rec-ollected that he had left a note for Char-ley saying he would be at home after six, and begging an immediate interview, the importance of which forbade any post-ponement.

"I wish I could come; but——" he began.

The chill smile swept over her face again, as she interrupted him:

"Don't come, if you don't want to."

"But I do want to come," he urged, "if I had not an engagement——"

"You need not make any excuse," she said frigidly.   "Your excuses are not so successful to-day that I care to hear them."

Stuyvesant wished that he could tell her that his engagement was with her brother, and that for her brother's sake he must keep it.   But it was impossible.

"Good-evening," she said, as she passed through the door, and the chill of those last words smote Stuyvesant to the heart.   It was the first time that he and she had parted except in amity; and a parting like this was hard to bear.

From the hospital he went directly to the College Club. He did not know when Charley would get his note, and when he might expect to see the boy. He must be prepared to wait, if need be, without leaving his apartment. He foresaw that he should have to forego his dinner if Charley did not return to the studio before night. Stuyvesant walked into the club and ordered a dozen raw oysters, as the food most easy to get and most easy for him to eat just then, when he felt as though a mouthful would choke him.

As he sat down at a table to give his order, little Mat Hitchcock came in, a man whom he detested.

"Hallo, Paul!" he cried, with a familiarity as offensive as it was unwarranted, "what's the matter with you? You look off-color to-night? Has your best girl gone back on you?"

Under the strain on Stuyvesant just then, this was more than he could stand.

He arose, and, facing Hitchcock, he said calmly, and yet with force:

"That is my business, Mr. Hitchcock, and I suggest that you mind your own."

Little Mat Hitchcock started back.

"I didn't mean to offend you," he said hastily.

"I think it likely," returned Paul coldly, "that you cannot help being offensive whether you mean it or not."

Hitchcock withdrew into the smoking-room, where he spent the evening telling everybody who chanced to come in how he had been grossly insulted by that Stuyvesant man.

When Paul had hastily swallowed his oysters, he left the Club and walked rapidly back to his apartment.

CHAPTER XI.

HE quaint little clock on the mantelpiece was chiming six as Stuyvesant let himself into his apartment and closed the door behind him. At any moment now Charley might be expected to make his appearance in answer to the note, and there was nothing for Paul to do but to wait. He lighted the gas, and proceeded to make up the fire, which had burned low.

After changing his costume to the ease of smoking-jacket and slippers, he filled his pipe.

In truth, his nerves had need of a seda-tive. Never had his composure received a ruder blow than it had that day. Now only, in the quiet of his own room, after he had in a measure recovered from the first shock of the discovery, could he real-

ize the full horror of the situation.   On
the discovery of the damning evidence of
the picture, all possibility of doubt had
fled, and with it all hope.   He groaned
inwardly, and strove to turn his thoughts
into a different channel.   When Charley
came, the situation must be faced boldly.
Explanations must be given and received.
Shifts and expedients must be devised.
It was a sickening prospect.   For the
moment surely he was entitled to indulge
in pleasanter reveries, if he could.

The little clock cut the silence with a
sharp, metallic voice.

Eight o'clock.   Even allowing Charley to have lingered over his dinner at
the Fried Cat or the Hole-in-the-Wall,
his favorite restaurants, where he met
many fellow-artists, long enough to have
smoked a cigar afterward, he could not
be much later now, unless he had gone
from his dinner straight to the theatre or
some place of amusement without stop-
ping at his studio.   How could he have
the heart to enjoy himself with Nemesis
on his track?   Stuyvesant felt a hot wave
of indignation against young Vaughn

roll across his mind. What right had Charley to be out among those joyous holiday throngs while he, Paul, was stretched on a rack of vicarious apprehensions? Was he to spend his evening, when he might have been with Kitty, when he should have been with Kitty, waiting for that boy, who did not even think it worth his while to return to his studio to see if anything had happened in his absence? "One would think," muttered Paul irefully, "that he would feel uneasy to-day, when the loss of the picture has just been discovered. It seems to me that if I were in his place I should not dare to leave that studio for a moment, knowing what it contains. But then if I had been in his place the Mary Magdalen would be in Sam Sargent's Paris apartments, where it belongs, and there would be none of this trouble at all."

Half-past twelve, within a minute or two, it was, when he glanced again at his watch. Was Charley never coming home? Was he—— And then for the first time an appalling thought swept across Paul's

consciousness like a spectre, and he shiv-
ered to his very marrow under the clutch
of his icy doubt. What if Charley never
came home again? What if he had
looked his last on the bright face that he
had learned to love so much? What if
Charley were dead?

No newspaper reader, no dweller and
worker in the busy hive of the metropolis,
is unfamiliar with the idea of suicide.
Like many another horror, it is a thing
to be lightly discussed and lightly dismissed, till we are brought into actual
contact with it, till one of our friends
bursts with his own hands the lock which
guards the great mystery. Then, indeed,
we realize what self-murder is, and always has been—a terrible exception im-
plying a burden of suffering, borne unsuspected until human nature could bear
it no longer, and flung aside then with
one rash gesture. And so it is that we
look on the suicide with the same pitying
wonder that we read of the tortures of the
Inquisition, and marvel that poor human-
ity can endure so much, and endure it so
long.

Of course Paul had no grounds to fear that Charley had taken the fatal step never to be retraced: he had misgivings only; but these misgivings grew with every moment that passed after the first chilling doubt had smitten him. Charley must have been leading a fearful life all these months, subjected to the exactions of a man like Zalinski, with the sword of this undiscovered secret suspended over his head by a hair which he could not but know must snap sooner or later. At last the sword had fallen; the secret had been discovered; and what was more likely than that the poor boy had accepted the swiftest and easiest solution of his difficulty, and had—— Paul shuddered. He knew that he had heard and read of many a suicide committed on slighter grounds than these.

He tore off his smoking-jacket and kicked off his slippers. He would go out; he would solve this horrible doubt if he could. But he paused even before he had taken his boots in his hands. It was long past one now. "The Rubens" would be locked up. Without a

11

key to the outer door, he could not get in; and he knew from experience that his chance of rousing any of the inmates would be small. Besides, there was a chance, a dim ghost of a chance, that Charley might yet come; and Stuyvesant had no right to be absent. It was better to wait till morning. He could act then; to-night he could do nothing but wait!

Stuyvesant had lost all count of the hours. The thronging thoughts that filled his brain annihilated all perception of time and space. He was like a man under a dose of hasheesh. He did not sleep, but he was conscious only in so far as he felt the dominant impression. How the long hours of that night wore away Paul could never tell, nor could he ever recall them without a shudder.

A piercing scream came up from the street. Perhaps a fight was in progress, or perhaps some poor creature had met with an accident. The cry partly roused Stuyvesant, and he stirred in his seat. Something fell to the ground. He had disturbed the manuscript of his book on Circumstantial Evidence, and it had dropped from the table. The closely written leaves lay at his feet in wild confusion. He did not move, but slowly consciousness came back to him. He was leaning his elbows on the table, and was gazing intently on Miss Vaughn's likeness. He had drawn the little curtains, but he had no recollection of the act, nor could he even remember taking that chair. Kitty had certainly not been in his thoughts, and yet here he was—and here, for aught he knew, he had been for hours—staring at her picture.

The eyes of the faithful portrait were looking into his, gently and pathetically. With a little stretch of fancy he could have imagined that they were filled with tears. His own, no doubt, were dim and weary. Poor Kitty! If it were indeed as he feared—if Charley, in his despair, had taken his life—she would never hold her head up again. But why pause for an "if"? Living or dead, there could be no doubt that Vaughn had stolen the Titian, and in that act alone there was measure enough of shame to bow his sister's head in the dust forever.

He glanced at the clock. It was ten minutes before six, and the fire had burned out to dull gray ashes. His first feeling of consternation at the thought that it was utterly hopeless to expect Charley now was succeeded by a sense of relief that the long night had worn itself away at last. It was morning.

More and more figures appeared on the street; and the lowering dawn broadened into a murky day. New York was awakening. Paul turned from the window and proceeded to get into his boots and overcoat. "The Rubens" might be open by this time. Still, he did not like to leave his room where he had waited so long. Suppose even now, by some unforeseen chance, Charley should come and find him absent? He would stay at his post to the end. Then his eye brightened a little as he hit on a simple expedient.

CHAPTER XII.

STUYVESANT stepped out into the little vestibule of his apartment and rang the District Messenger call which was fixed at one side of the door. Then he returned to his room and sat down to his desk. He wrote a very urgent letter to Charley. It was a relief to him to write it; it seemed to give him an assurance that his friend was still in the land of the living. He asked if his note of the night before had not been received, and begged Charley, if he was at home, to come over without losing an instant. "It is of the greatest importance," he wrote, and he signed himself "Ever your friend, Paul Stuyvesant." If Charley were there to read it, he hoped that he would understand that *ever* as conveying an assurance that Paul would stand by him to the end.

In due course the messenger-boy returned.   Paul's ashen lips could hardly
falter out the monosyllable " Well?" for
he knew that the doubts and fears which
had possessed him during fourteen hours
of a mental strain such as he had never
before undergone were to be resolved now
—for better, it might be; it could scarcely
be for worse.   But the boy seemed un-
concerned enough.

"Gen'leman was in bed," he said, and
he handed Paul a note.

" In bed?" echoed Stuyvesant, as he
reeled into a seat with the unopened letter in his hand.   " In bed?" he repeated.
" When did he get home?"

"Dunno," answered the boy, with a
grin; and then Paul realized that the best
thing he could do would be to read the
answer, which was addressed in Charley's
handwriting.   He tore open the envelope
and read the following, written in pencil
on the back of his own note:

"DEAR OLD POST SCRIPT: Of course
I found your note last night when I got
home; but as it was after midnight then,

I never thought you would expect me till the morning by the bright light. I'd have run around right off if I had supposed you would let me in. I hope you haven't been getting into trouble with the police, and want me to bail you out? You can count on me every time. You can even count on me this time, as soon as I can hustle myself into a few garments. I trust your business is not serious; though I fear it is, since you rouse me out of my beauty sleep so recklessly. When you have said your say, I've something to tell you about myself which may interest you. I think it will—and I know it will surprise you.

"Yours in the bath-tub,

"C. V."

Paul dismissed the messenger with a nod and stared at the letter in his hand as if it were a cryptogram. What could it mean? It was couched in the writer's habitual tone of careless raillery. There was nothing mysterious or morbid or melodramatic about it: it was just such a note as the boy might have written if

there were no Zalinski in the world and
if the Mary Magdalen still rested in its
proper frame. Could he have been
dreaming? Stuyvesant asked himself if
it was nothing but a nightmare springing
from the hideous watch he had kept.
He found no solace in this idea: he knew
his head was all right, even if his nerves
were shaken; and he turned to the letter
again with a profound bewilderment.
" I've something to tell you about myself
which may interest you. I think it will—
and I know it will surprise you." This
was the only sentence that seemed in the
least out of the common. These were
the only words that even hinted at a mystery. But that Charley would refer to a
matter of such gravity in such a banter-
ing strain was impossible.

So his long night's vigil had been
wasted. Charley had returned home at
midnight, and then had thought it was
too late to come around. Paul grew
angry as he recollected how many wake-
ful hours he had spent since twelve
o'clock, and how there had not been one
of them in which Charley's appearance

would not have been hailed as a relief. But Charley had been in bed and asleep all the time; and he grumbled now because he had been disturbed an hour too early in the morning.

Paul's wrath waxed hotter and hotter, and it was not far from the boiling-point when the door opened and Charley walked in.

He was neat, spruce, and well-dressed as ever, rosy from cold water and the January air. About him there were no traces of a sleepless night and no signs of a hurried toilet. Everything was in place, even to a little hothouse flower in his buttonhole, which might have been culled that moment, so fresh and fragrant did it look.

He came in jauntingly with his dripping umbrella in his hand and deposited it carelessly in the corner. The water ran down and collected in a little pool on the carpet.

"Morning, morning," he said. "Halloo! what's up? You look as if you had been sitting up all night with your own corpse."

"I have not been to bed," answered Paul. He could not go on. The young fellow's appearance was in too sharp a contrast to the fears that had been torturing him.

"Dissipating, eh?" continued Charley lightly, and then, noticing the other's continued gravity: "What are you looking so cross about? Oh, I see! I've left my umbrella dripping! Well, I never can remember." He took it up and stood it in the rack. "I won't be guilty again. Now, tell me what's the row?"

"Charley," said Paul, with an effort, "I have something very serious to talk about; but you mentioned in your note that you had something to tell me. Perhaps it is the same thing. Go on. You may tell me everything."

Charley stared at him with unfeigned amazement. "I don't see how it can be the same thing," he said. "You don't know anything about it, unless you are a sharper fellow than I take you for."

"Perhaps I am sharper than you take me for, and clews have come to my hand which you never could have dreamed of. So go on; let me hear all about it."

"Let's hear what's worrying you first, old fellow," said Charley, with real concern. "Something has happened; I can see that: you look as white as a ghost with the dyspepsia. You haven't been sitting up all night and sending off for me at cockcrow for nothing. What's the matter? Anything about Kitty?"

Paul fired up at once. "Don't dare to mention her name!" he said hotly.

"Come, that's cool," rejoined Charley. "Pray, why mayn't I mention my own sister's name? She isn't yours yet, and I doubt if she ever would be if she heard you talk to me like that."

"No trifling," retorted Stuyvesant. "I know all."

Charley's eyes opened wider, and the corners of his mouth seemed twitching with a desire to laugh; but he only said:

"The deuce you do! What a lot you must know, then!"

Paul had hard work to keep his temper. To him this cavalier way of treating a serious matter was incomprehensible. Steadying his voice with an effort, he said:

"I am deeply pained to see you approach this subject in so flippant a spirit. I was in your studio yesterday."

"Yes, and you left a note there. I got it. What's that to do with it?"

"While in your studio, I looked round among the pictures; I searched everywhere——"

"Cool of you; but, considering who you are, I'll forgive you this time," said Charley, who was engaged in lighting a cigarette.

"In the farthest angle under the gallery I came on the Mary Magdalen."

Charley's lips were puckered into a whistle.

"Now, do you know," he said finally, "I'm sorry you found that, old man. I hadn't intended you to see it—at least, not yet. I meant to have—— Well, no matter; it's none the worse, I suppose."

Paul's astonishment at this reception of his information was well-nigh ludicrous. He almost gasped for breath, and he stared at Charley as if the artist were a being of some new and undescribed species.

"How did you gain access to Mr. Sargent's apartments?" he at last found voice to ask.

"With a silver key. I never met an incorruptible concierge in my life," answered the young fellow, with a light laugh.

"And can you speak of it in that tone? Do you not realize what you have done? Do you make no account of your mother and sister—the shame and misery you may bring on them——"

"Come, come, Stuyvesant," said Charley quickly; "that's pitching it rather too strong."

"I can't speak half as strongly as I feel," answeerd Paul hotly. "I think the whole transaction as mean and despicable as anything I ever heard of. I——"

"Look here, Mr. Stuyvesant," interrupted the young man, rising and standing before him, "you are going too far. So just pull up short where you are, will you?"

"What did you come here to tell me?" asked Paul. "Be candid and above-board now, and I'll do what I can for you."

"What I came here to tell you is purely my own business," answered Charley stiffly. "I should have been very glad to tell you about it, but I don't think it would possess the interest for you now that once I had a fancy it would. At any rate, after the words you have used to me, I should have no pleasure in telling it."

The young man picked up his umbrella and turned toward the door. Paul could not suffer him to leave like this, with no conception of the magnitude of the crime he had committed.

"Don't go yet," he said. "You don't seem to realize that this is a very serious matter. Do you know that this is nothing more nor less than a theft you have committed?"

"I do not regard it in that light at all," answered Charley, with his hand on the lock of the door; "and, since you entertain that opinion of me, the less we see of each other in the future the better. Good-morning."

The door slammed with a vicious sound, and Paul was alone.

An hour later Stuyvesant stood on a street-corner with his watch in his hand, wondering whether he could yet venture to call on Miss Vaughn.

CHAPTER XIII.

IT still lacked several minutes of half-past ten—more minutes than he cared to count—when Stuyvesant stood on the steps of Mrs. Vaughn's house and pulled the bell. He had never before called on Kitty at so early an hour, except by previous appointment, when it had been arranged that he was to be her escort on some excursion demanding a start betimes. But this morning he felt an imperative need of seeing the girl he loved. He wanted the solace of her presence, the comfort of a few minutes' conversation with her, after his long night of agony and his very peculiar interview with Charley at the end of it. He felt that he could not talk to her on the subject that was uppermost in his thoughts. He

170

was determined to work out her brother's salvation alone, if that were possible; and till the last moment he would keep from the sister all knowledge of the terrible facts he had discovered.   But he wanted to see Kitty for another reason. They had parted in coolness the night before; and this was in itself no slight addition to the burden he was called upon to bear.   He could not believe that she was angry with him still; at any rate, a complete humiliation on his part, and unstinted apology, even without an explanation, would doubtless serve to smooth the matter over.

When the servant opened the door, he inquired for Miss Vaughn.   Could he see her?

"Oh, yes, of course; she is upstairs now with Mr. Charles."

This was an unexpected embarrassment.   Paul had no desire to meet Charley again—at least, not just at present. He hesitated for a full minute, and a very little would have tempted him to run away.   However, Stuyvesant's was not a shrinking nature, and he entered

12

the house and sent a message to Miss Vaughn. Would she see him alone for a few minutes?

He was shown into Kitty's special room, the same in which he had waited for her on the previous day—the same in which he had waited for her more times than he could reckon, though every time had its own sweet memories. The apartment was full of remembrances of her; the evidences of the girl's *dilettante* art were scattered around in picturesque confusion.

Stuyvesant was at a loss to account for Charley's early visit to his mother's house, where of late he had not been a frequent visitor at the best of times. Just now one would have supposed that he had enough to think of and to do, under present circumstances, without making morning calls. But Charley's conduct in this crisis had been systematically unaccountable. It was impossible to predict what he would do or say, what he would leave undone or unsaid.

The door opened, and Miss Vaughn entered. She looked very dainty and winsome in a fresh morning-gown; her eyes were dancing with happiness and health; and she had a bewitching smile on her lips. She tried to frown as Paul arose, but the smile was rebellious and would not down, so she gave up her vain assumption of displeasure and broke into a merry laugh.

"Well, Bear," she said, "have you come to apologize for your rudeness last night?"

This was just the reception Paul wished for. He was willing to apologize. Metaphorically speaking, he asked nothing better than to grovel at her little feet. All he was unwilling to do was to explain; and Kitty did not ask for an explanation.

He managed even to say, with a fair attempt at a light manner:

"If you call me a bear, you must expect to be hugged."

"Hands off!" she cried, retreating behind a chair. "I haven't forgiven you yet for being cross."

"I throw myself on your mercy," he said, "and I beg you to believe that I was the greatest sufferer by not being on hand to walk home with you yesterday evening."

"Of course you were," she answered. "People who let their tempers get the best of them are always the greatest sufferers in the long run. But, now you have come back in a proper frame of mind, you shall be forgiven, and I'll let you take the kiss of peace."

And he took it at once. It seemed to refresh him.

"The fact is," she went on, "I have just heard something so interesting and so exciting that it has driven everything else out of my head, and it is impossible for me to bear malice. You shall guess what it is."

Paul could not guess. He had not the spirits for badinage, and, after one or two futile efforts under pressure of her insistence, he gave it up.

"Well, then," she said, "be prepared. Catch hold of something. Charley has been with me all the morning, and he has made a full confession."

Kitty's recommendation to catch hold

of something had not been unnecessary. Paul fairly reeled under her announcement. Charley had told her; and now, instead of Stuyvesant finding her crushed and spirit-broken by the confession, she met him with a laugh on her lips, and referred to it as something "exciting and interesting."

"He has told you all?" he gasped.

"Yes; everything. Isn't it just too lovely?"

Paul stared.

"It accounts for all that has been puzzling us in his ways of late."

It certainly did account for Charley's change of habits; but Stuyvesant could not share Miss Vaughn's satisfaction.

"You don't seem pleased," she said more coldly. "Perhaps you're jealous. Oh, I haven't forgotten how you raved about Gladys Tennant's beauty yesterday, when you met her in the street-car, though you pretended you didn't know her."

At any other time Paul would have asked no better pastime than to combat this pretty, unreasonable pique; but now all his faculties were absorbed in a boundless bewilderment. What Miss Tennant had to do with the matter he tried vainly to guess.

"Oh, yes, you look very innocent and unconscious," pursued Kitty. "But there, I am too happy; I can't be angry with you, even when you deserve it. Why, you dear old stupid, when you met Gladys she was on her way to take the 3:30 train home to Yonkers. She had very good reason to suppose Charley might happen to be on the same train; and sure enough he was on it; and the whole thing was settled as they walked from the station to her house; and he dined and spent the evening at Mr. Tennant's in the character of—in what character, do you suppose?"

Paul could not hazard an opinion.

"How perversely stupid you are this morning!" she said, with a frown of impatience. "Haven't I told you as plainly as words could say it that Charley proposed to Gladys Tennant yesterday, and was accepted, and—— What's the matter now?"

"Is that all Charley told you?" he asked.

"Yes, that is all; and a very sufficient piece of news it is, too, for a rainy morning, I should think," she retorted.

Paul breathed again. The fatal secret was still unsuspected by Kitty.

"You are not very profuse in your congratulations," she went on, after a moment's pause. Then she looked at him more closely. "What's the matter, Paul? You look tired and troubled; you are not yourself this morning. Aren't you well, dear?"

There was a note of infinite tenderness and feeling in her voice, and Paul caught the hand that she passed caressingly over his brow and pressed it to his lips.

"There's nothing the matter with me," he said. "I had a rather disturbed night, that's all. Some—something's happened to worry me. Tell me, though: this engagement—it's rather sudden, isn't it? I didn't know that Charley was paying attention in that quarter."

"Neither did I. None of us did," answered she. "He has been most preter-

naturally sly about it, hasn't he? You
see, it seems he has been in love quite a
while. As far as I can make out, she
took him into camp on the boat; you
know they came back from Europe on the
same steamer last fall, and he has been
sinking deeper and deeper into love ever
since, until now he is over head and ears.
But he had an idea that Gladys was fond
of some other fellow, and it has made
him very miserable. He never hoped
that anything would come of it, so he
never told a soul a word about it. Finally, he made up his mind that something had to be done in a hurry; so he
took the plunge yesterday, and he found
out that Gladys has been sighing for him
as long as he has been dying for her, and
now everything is lovely."

"I see," said Paul slowly.

He understood now the nature of the
communication which Charley had intended to make to him that morning.
He saw they had been at cross-purposes.
He thought that the young artist had
chosen a very inopportune moment for
his wooing. The selfishness which Char-

ley displayed in drawing a young girl's bright life into the shadow of his own struck Paul painfully. It was of a piece with the incomprehensible indifference and levity with which he had treated the whole transaction.

"Well, you are not very enthusiastic," said Kitty, after a pause.

"Of course I wish him all possible happiness," said Paul with an effort, for the words seemed to stick in his throat.

"You shall say it to his face, then," said Miss Vaughn, running to the door.

She was in the hall in an instant, and calling with her clear, high-pitched voice:

"Charley, Charley! Come here a minute; I want you."

"Kitty, I beg of you——" Paul cried, springing to his feet.

But the summons had already gone forth. It was impossible to check this young lady in any course she had resolved on; and Paul had no possible excuse for his unwillingness to meet her brother. It was evident that Charley had told her nothing of their quarrel in the morning. Stuyvesant could only remain passive, and let things take their course.

Presently Charley entered, light-hearted and lively as ever, without the trace of a care on his face. Paul, in his embarrassment, had withdrawn into the recess of the window.

"Well, Kit, what is it?" said the young fellow as he came in.

"Oh, I've just called you down to receive Paul's congratulations. I've told him all about it—— Why, where is he?"

"Thanks, I'll take Stuyvesant's felicitations for granted," said Charley coolly. "You see, they probably would not be exuberantly overflowing. He's been engaged long enough himself to have found out that it isn't a subject for unmixed congratulations!"

Kitty's quick eye detected something strained in the situation.

"What's the matter with you two?" she said. "Have you been quarrelling?"

"Well, it's this way," said Charley. "Stuyvesant has just found out about the Mary Magdalen; and the manner in which

I secured it seems to have jarred with his fine sense of honor."

Paul nearly fainted. So her brother had told Kitty the whole business, after all. There was nothing more to conceal. He came forward from the window, just as Kitty answered:

"Well, you know, Charley, I did not think it exactly *nice* myself."

Was the whole Vaughn family destitute of the moral sense? The girl he was engaged to referred to a felony as not "exactly *nice!*"

"That's a matter of opinion," said Charley calmly.

Paul disagreed with him, but he said nothing.

"If a man chooses to hide away a masterpiece like that, the outside world must get at it as they can," the artist said.

Paul still remained silent.

"Well, there's something in that," said Kitty, appealing to him.

"Perhaps there is," said Stuyvesant stiffly. "I can't see it myself. To take away Mr. Sargent's picture without his knowledge is, in my eyes, nothing more nor less than a theft."

"Since Mr. Sargent has been lucky enough to recover his Titian," said Charley, "I think he will be charitable enough to find a milder word for my very petty larceny."

"Recovered his Titian?" cried Paul in amazement. "How can that be?"

"By the exertions of the very intelligent and efficient police of the good city of Paris," answered Charley.

"Haven't you read the papers yet?" he continued. "You were up early enough this morning."

"No: I have—I have been thinking of something else," said Paul, producing the *Gotham Gazette* from his pocket, still folded as he had taken it from his table.

Charley took the paper from him and opened it.

"Read that," he said, indicating a paragraph in the cable news.

With growing amazement, Paul read this despatch:

"A PICTURE RESTORED——
"TO ITS OWNER!

"MR. SAM SARGENT RECOVERS HIS MARY MAGDALEN.

"PARIS, January 3. — The Parisian police have done a bit of detective work worthy of the real Vidocq or the fabled Lecoq. They have caught the man who cut Mr. Sargent's Titian from its frame yesterday, and they have got back the picture itself. As I telegraphed you last night, they had a clew; and so adroitly did they follow it up, that they laid hands on the thief within twelve hours after the robbery had been discovered. The theft was committed by a single man, an employee of the low curiosity-shop where the picture was discovered two years ago. He bribed the concierge of Mr. Sargent's apartments yesterday morning, and the painting was cut from its frame only an hour or two before the owner returned. The rascal has made a full confession, in which he acknowledges that his motive was to hold the Mary Magdalen to ransom, and to strike the American owner

for a hundred thousand francs.   Luckily,
a sharp-eyed detective remarked the un-
easiness of the concierge when Mr. Sargent announced his loss.   Under pressure, the concierge supplied a description
of the thief, and the police ran him down
at once.   Mr. Sargent has sent ten thousand francs to the Hôtel-Dieu to endow a
special bed for the detective department
of the police."

"So, you see, Mr. Sam Sargent is in far
too good a humor this morning to be very
angry with me," said Charley, when he
had finished.

"The Mary Magdalen recovered?   In
Paris?"   Paul was stupefied with amazement.   "Then what was it I saw in your
room yesterday?"

Charley stared at him blankly.   Grad-
ually a light seemed to dawn on his mind,
and the hard lines of his face thawed out.
Finally, the whole situation burst upon
him at once, and he fell back on the sofa,
where he rolled helplessly in uncontrol-
lable merriment.

"Why, you don't mean to say you

thought *that* was the original?" he gasped, as soon as he could recover his breath.

"I certainly did," said Paul gravely.

The humor of the affair had not yet dawned upon him.

"Oh, this will be the death of me!" said Charley, in the intervals of his merriment. "Here is an unlooked-for testimonial to the merits of my medium! I shall publish it, Paul—I certainly shall; and then I'll take a big studio and turn out old masters by the gross."

He was obliged to stop, choking with laughter.

"I do not understand," said Kitty.

"Why, it's this way," continued Charley, who had temporarily regained command of his voice. "As I told you, I bribed the concierge and made a copy of Sargent's Mary Magdalen. Sargent is a good friend of mine, but I couldn't get at him to ask his permission; so I just did without it. I knew that there wasn't a government in Europe that wouldn't let me go through its galleries and copy what I liked. I primed my own

canvas, as I always do, and I used my
famous medium; and really it made a
very respectable old master indeed.   It
would pass muster anywhere—wouldn't
it, Paul?"

There was a fresh explosion of laughter,
and then the young fellow resumed:

"I kept it as shady as I could, for I
intended it as a wedding-present for you
two; but Master Paul, here, must go
hunting after a mare's nest, and find one
with an addled egg in it.   When he got
pitching into me about the theft, and so
forth, I supposed he was referring to the
underhand way in which I secured my
copy, and for which my conscience has
pricked me a little more than once, I confess; but I've written the whole story to
Sargent, and I'm sure he'll say it's all
right.   But Paul actually thought I had
gone in with a crape mask and an ink-
eraser, and cut the picture out of the
frame!   Oh, I shall die of this, I know
I shall!"

"And did you think my brother capa-
ble——" began Kitty indignantly.

"Oh, don't, Kit! Don't scold him,"

said Charley. " The poor fellow has had the worst of it all through."

Stuyvesant looked from one to the other in silence.

" Tell me, Paul," Charley continued, " how did you ever get on the track of the Mary Magdalen at all? Did you find it by accident?"

" No," said Paul. His mind was still whirling with the astonishing developments of the morning, and he could not force his ideas out of the beaten track. " No," he said, " I learned that you had been paying money at different times to a man named Zalinski, who turned out to be——"

" A pawnbroker," interrupted Charley. " One by one my cherished secrets shrivel up under the eagle eye of my future brother-in-law. I have dealt with Zalinski; I buy most of my curios and studio properties from him. I got that guillotine-knife that hangs in your sitting-room from Zalinski, and the bowie-knife too. I have even left him a standing order to let me know whenever he comes across anything that may appeal to my outland-

13

ish taste; but I don't tell people of it. For one thing, it looks shady to deal at a pawnshop; and for another, if the rest of the boys tumbled to my racket, Zalinski's prices would go up, and there wouldn't be so much left for me."

"Charley," said Paul, advancing with outstretched hand, "I have made a great fool of myself, and my doubt of you was an outrage. Can you forgive me?"

"With all my heart, old boy, especially as you've given me the best laugh I've had for years."

"And you, Kitty?" said he, turning to Miss Vaughn.

"I don't know. I'll consider it. You've no business to be so suspicious," she anwered, putting her hands behind her.

"I'll try and be less so in the future," he answered humbly.

"And you'd better look out and walk the matrimonial chalk-line without wobbling, Miss Kitty," said her brother; "for you'll have a husband that could give Vidocq long odds and beat him."

"I think, on the whole, as you are

penitent, I'll forgive you," said Kitty gravely, wholly ignoring her brother's irreverent observation. "Now I'm going to Yonkers with Charley to kiss Gladys Tennant. You can come if you want."

"You can come, but you can't kiss," interjected Charley.

"I'd like it of all things," said Paul eagerly.

"You'll see how nice she is to talk to when you know who she is," said young Vaughn mischievously; "and when you get back you can sit down and write a nice long chapter on the fallacies of circumstantial evidence, as exemplified in the personal experience of the author."

THE END.

RECENT ISSUES IN APPLETONS' TOWN AND COUNTRY LIBRARY.

THE FLIGHT OF THE SHADOW. By GEORGE MACDONALD, author of "Malcolm," "Annals of a Quiet Neighborhood," etc. 12mo. Paper, 50 cents; cloth, $1.00.

"It is extremely entertaining, contains a charming love-story, and is beautifully written, like everything from Mr. MacDonald's pen."—*St. Paul Pioneer-Press.*

LOVE OR MONEY. By KATHARINE LEE, author of "A Western Wildflower," "In London Town," etc. 12mo. Paper, 50 cents; cloth, $1.00.

"In point of cleverness this novel is quite up to the standard of the excellent Town and Country Library in which it appears. Most of the characters are well drawn, and there are some singularly strong scenes in the book."—*Charleston News and Courier.*

NOT ALL IN VAIN. By ADA CAMBRIDGE, author of "The Three Miss Kings," "My Guardian," etc. 12mo. Paper, 50 cents; cloth, $1.00.

"A worthy companion to the best of the author's former efforts, and in some respects superior to any of them."—*Detroit Free Press.*

"A better story has not been published in many moons."—*Philadelphia Inquirer.*

IT HAPPENED YESTERDAY. By FREDERICK MARSHALL, author of "Claire Brandon." 12mo. Paper, 50 cents; cloth, $1.00.

"An odd, fantastic tale, whose controlling agency is an occult power which the world thus far has doubted and wondered at alternately rather than studied."—*Chicago Times.*

"A psychological story of very powerful interest."—*Boston Home Journal.*

MY GUARDIAN. By ADA CAMBRIDGE, author of "The Three Miss Kings," "Not All in Vain," etc. 12mo. Paper, 50 cents; cloth, $1.00.

"A story which will, from first to last, enlist the sympathies of the reader by its simplicity of style and fresh, genuine feeling. . . . The author is *au fait* at the delineation of character."—*Boston Transcript.*

"The *dénoûment* is all that the most ardent romance-reader could desire."—*Chicago Evening Journal.*

ELINE VERE. By Louis Couperus. Translated from the Dutch by J. T. Grein. With an Introduction by Edmund Gosse. Holland Fiction Series. 12mo. Cloth, $1.00.

"The established authorities in art and literature retain their exclusive place in dictionaries and hand-books long after the claim of their juniors to be observed with attention has been practically conceded at home. For this reason, partly, and partly also because the mental life of Holland receives little attention in this country, no account has yet been taken of the revolution in Dutch taste which has occupied the last six or seven years. I believe that the present occasion is the first on which it has been brought to the notice of any English-speaking public. . . . 'Eline Vere' is an admirable performance."—Edmund Gosse, *in Introduction.*

"Most careful in its details of description, most picturesque in its coloring."—*Boston Post.*

"A vivacious and skillful performance, giving an evidently faithful picture of society, and evincing the art of a true story-teller."—*Philadelphia Telegraph.*

"Those who associate Dutch characters and Dutch thought with ideas of the purely phlegmatic, will read with astonishment and pleasure the oft-times stirring and passionate sentences of this novel."—*Public Opinion.*

"The *dénoûment* is tragical, thrilling, and picturesque."—*New York World.*

"If modern Dutch literature has other books as good as this to offer, we hope that they will soon find a translator."—*Chicago Evening Journal.*

A PURITAN PAGAN. By Julien Gordon, author of "A Diplomat's Diary," etc. 12mo. Cloth, $1.00.

"Mrs. Van Rensselaer Cruger grows stronger as she writes. . . . The lines in her story are boldly and vigorously etched."—*New York Times.*

"The author's recent books have made for her a secure place in current literature, where she can stand fast. . . . Her latest production, 'A Puritan Pagan,' is an eminently clever story, in the best sense of the word clever."—*Philadelphia Telegraph.*

"Has already made its mark as a popular story, and will have an abundance of readers. . . . It contains some useful lessons that will repay the thoughtful study of persons of both sexes."—*New York Journal of Commerce.*

"This brilliant novel will without doubt add to the repute of the writer who chooses to be known as Julien Gordon. . . . The ethical purpose of the author is kept fully in evidence through a series of intensely interesting situations."—*Boston Beacon.*

"It is obvious that the author is thoroughly at home in illustrating the manner and the sentiment of the best society of both America and Europe."—*Chicago Times.*

New York: D. APPLETON & CO., 1, 3, & 5 Bond Street.

ON THE PLANTATION. By JOEL CHANDLER HARRIS, author of "Uncle Remus." With 23 Illustrations by E. W. KEMBLE, and Portrait of the Author. 12mo. Cloth, $1.50.

"The book is in the characteristic vein which has made the author so famous and popular as an interpreter of plantation character."—*Rochester Union and Advertiser.*

"Those who never tire of Uncle Remus and his stories—with whom we would be accounted—will delight in Joe Maxwell and his exploits."—*London Saturday Review.*

"Altogether a most charming book."—*Chicago Times.*

"Really a valuable, if modest, contribution to the history of the civil war within the Confederate lines, particularly on the eve of the catastrophe. Two or three new animal fables are introduced with effect; but the history of the plantation, the printing-office, the black runaways, and white deserters, of whom the impending break-up made the community tolerant, the coon and fox hunting, forms the serious purpose of the book, and holds the reader's interest from beginning to end."—*New York Evening Post.*

UNCLE REMUS: His Songs and his Sayings. The Folk-lore of the Old Plantation. By JOEL CHANDLER HARRIS. Illustrated from Drawings by F. S. CHURCH and J. H. MOSER, of Georgia. 12mo. Cloth, $1.50.

"The idea of preserving and publishing these legends, in the form in which the old plantation negroes actually tell them, is altogether one of the happiest literary conceptions of the day. And very admirably is the work done. . . . In such touches lies the charm of this fascinating little volume of legends, which deserves to be placed on a level with *Reincke Fuchs* for its quaint humor, without reference to the ethnological interest possessed by these stories, as indicating, perhaps, a common origin for very widely severed races."—*London Spectator.*

"We are just discovering what admirable literary material there is at home, what a great mine there is to explore, and how quaint and peculiar is the material which can be dug up. Mr. Harris's book may be looked on in a double light—either as a pleasant volume recounting the stories told by a typical old colored man to a child, or as a valuable contribution to our somewhat meager folk-lore. . . . To Northern readers the story of Brer (Brother—Brudder) Rabbit may be novel. To those familiar with plantation life, who have listened to these quaint old stories, who have still tender reminiscences of some good old mauma who told these wondrous adventures to them when they were children, Brer Rabbit, the Tar Baby, and Brer Fox come back again with all the past pleasures of younger days."—*New York Times.*

"Uncle Remus's sayings on current happenings are very shrewd and bright, and the plantation and revival songs are choice specimens of their sort."—*Boston Journal.*

New York: D. APPLETON & CO., 1, 3, & 5 Bond Street.

THE LAST WORDS OF THOMAS CARLYLE.

Including *Wotton Reinfred*, Carlyle's only essay in fiction ; the *Excursion (Futile Enough) to Paris ;* and letters from Thomas Carlyle, also letters from Mrs. Carlyle, to a personal friend. With Portrait. 12mo. Cloth, gilt top, $1.75.

"The interest of 'Wotton Reinfred' to me is considerable, from the sketches which it contains of particular men and women, most of whom I knew and could, if necessary, identify. The story, too, is taken generally from real life, and perhaps Carlyle did not finish it, from the sense that it could not be published while the persons and things could be recognized. That objection to the publication no longer exists. Everybody is dead whose likenesses have been drawn, and the incidents stated have long been forgotten."—JAMES ANTHONY FROUDE.

"'Wotton Reinfred' is interesting as a historical document. It gives Carlyle before he had adopted his peculiar manner, and yet there are some characteristic bits—especially at the beginning—in the Sartor Resartus vein. I take it that these are reminiscences of Irving and of the Thackeray circle, and there is a curious portrait of Coleridge, not very thinly veiled. There is enough autobiography, too, of interest in its way."—LESLIE STEPHEN.

"No complete edition of the Sage of Chelsea will be able to ignore these manuscripts."—*Pall Mall Gazette.*

MEN, MINES, AND ANIMALS IN SOUTH AFRICA. By Lord RANDOLPH S. CHURCHILL.

With Portrait, Sixty five Illustrations, and a Map. 8vo. 337 pages. Cloth, $5.00.

"The subject-matter of the book is of unsurpassed interest to all who either travel in new countries, to see for themselves the new civilizations, or follow closely the experiences of such travelers. And Lord Randolph's eccentricities are by no means such as to make his own reports of what he saw in the new states of South Africa any the less interesting than his active eyes and his vigorous pen naturally make them."—*Brooklyn Eagle.*

"Lord Randolph Churchill's pages are full of diversified adventures and experience, from any part of which interesting extracts could be collected. . . . A thoroughly attractive book."—*London Telegraph.*

"Provided with amusing illustrations, which always fall short of caricature, but perpetually suggest mirthful entertainment."—*Philadelphia Ledger.*

"The book is the better for having been written somewhat in the line of journalism. It is a volume of travel containing the results of a journalist's trained observation and intelligent reflection upon political affairs. Such a work is a great improvement upon the ordinary book of travel. Lord Randolph Churchill thoroughly enjoyed his experiences in the African bush, and has produced a record of his journey and exploration which has hardly a dull page in it."—*New York Tribune.*

www.ingramcontent.com/pod-product-compliance
Lightning Source LLC
Chambersburg PA
CBHW032009060726
47497CB00017B/2413